it's in his forever

SHELLY ALEXANDER

ALSO BY SHELLY ALEXANDER

Shelly's titles with a little less steam (still sexy, though!):

The Red River Valley Series

It's In His Heart – Coop & Ella's Story

It's In His Touch – Blake & Angelique's Story

It's In His Smile – Talmadge & Miranda's Story

It's In His Arms – Mitchell & Lorenda's Story

It's In His Forever - Langston & His Secret Love's Story

It's In His Song - Dylan & Hailey's Story

It's In His Christmas Wish - Ross & Kimberly's Story

The Angel Fire Falls Series

Dare Me Once — Trace & Lily's Story

Dare Me Again — Elliott & Rebel's Story

Dare Me Now - TBA

Dare Me Always - TBA

Shelly's sizzling titles (with a lot of steam):

The Checkmate Inc. Series

ForePlay – Leo & Chloe's Story

Rookie Moves – Dex & Ava's Story

Get Wilde – Ethan & Adeline's Story

Sinful Games – Oz & Kendall's Story

Wilde Rush - Jacob & Grace's Story TBA

To my husband. You've been my forever since the day I met you.

And to my niece, Connie.
Thank you for helping me plot this story.

CHAPTER ONE

Only in Red River would the city council meet in a saloon.

Sandra Edwards tried to keep her voice steady and confident as the council members stared at her with blank expressions. Because it was Monday morning, Cotton Eyed Joe's—Red River's favorite watering hole—was empty, besides a few busy employees who were getting ready for the lunch crowd. So, the council thought it would be perfect for an emergency meeting.

The Irish liqueur Chairperson Clydelle requested in her morning coffee probably had something to do with the meeting location, too.

Sandra squared her shoulders. "The extreme snowboarding championship is just two weeks away, and we're ready." Red River had gotten plenty of snow; every inn, bed and breakfast, and hotel in town was booked solid. The best snowboarders around the globe would start arriving soon for practice runs before the competition began. "There's just one issue we need to address, which is why I asked to speak to you first thing this morning."

As the event coordinator who'd brought the competition to Red River after the previous location had to withdraw due to lack of snowfall, it was her job to keep the council up to date, but she did *not* want to give them the news. Convincing the council to host an event of such magnitude right there in the small vacation town of Red River, and on short notice, hadn't been easy. It had taken a lot of assurances that she wouldn't let anything go wrong. A lot of promises that she wouldn't allow the event to become a black mark that could deter Red River's booming tourism. A lot of guarantees that she could and would make the competition a smashing success.

She'd meant every assurance, every promise, every guarantee. Even if no one else in Red River had confidence in her tarnished reputation, *she* was confident that she could pull off the enormous undertaking.

Until late last night.

A sixtyish man wearing flannel and a camouflage, winter duck hunting hat with flaps covering both ears braced his elbows against the rustic wood table. "We heard about your problem," said Councilman Flaps.

Of course, they had.

Sandra's sharp breath whistled through the small part between her lips.

Why had she bothered to hope to do damage control by delivering the news herself? News traveled faster in a small mountain town than a world class snowboarder on a downhill course during the winter Olympics.

She cleared her throat. "Yes, well—"

"You've lost your safety officer for the event," said Councilwoman Maureen. She was a tough cookie who didn't put up with nonsense, and had been the receptionist at the sheriff's office for years. Probably why she got away with wearing a sweatshirt that read "I've got beautiful granddaughters. I've also got a gun, a shovel, and an alibi."

They were already referring to the problem as Sandra's. Message received. She had to come up with a solution, and fast, if she wanted to pull off the event and collect her big payday so she could start her life over somewhere else.

Anywhere else.

She laced her fingers in front of her as she stood facing the council. "Dr. Wells took an unfortunate tumble on the slopes." The International Snowboarding Association guidelines required a safety officer be present during the event who had both first aid knowledge and skill on the slopes. Cooper Wells—Red River's only chiropractor—had agreed. Unfortunately, his expertise as a black diamond skier hadn't stopped a reckless teen from blindsiding him during the annual midnight downhill torch parade.

Another councilman in a cowboy hat snorted. "Unfortunate tumble? I heard he needs several surgeries, metal pins to piece the bones in his leg back together, and at least a few months of physical therapy so he doesn't walk with a limp the rest of his life."

That description seemed like the very definition of *unfortunate* to Sandra.

She nodded. "It's horrible, but his wife called me last night. Ella and Coop said the show must go on." Sandra waved both hands in the air like she was in show biz and did her best to flash a dazzling smile.

Every last council member kept a poker face.

Even scarier, not one of them blinked.

Sandra seriously considered breaking into a tap dance just to get a reaction.

Slowly, Chairperson Clydelle raised her spiked coffee to her lips and sipped. Then she hiccupped and covered her mouth with her fingertips.

And the locals called *Sandra's* character into question for something that happened eons ago. Something she hadn't done, but had taken the blame to protect her father.

For all the good it had done her. The jerk still left her and her mom flat broke, never paid a dime of child support, and bounced from one pharmacy job to the next throughout the Southwest. Target-rich environments for a pharmacist who was addicted to pain killers.

Sandra drew in a breath and plowed on. "I've already got feelers out to bring in a new safety officer. Taos isn't that far from

Red River. They have a much bigger pool of medical professionals." She kept her tone warm and confident. "And because they're as..." She covered her mouth with a fist before choking out the next word. "...*blessed* as we are to live in the southern Rockies, many are seasoned skiers with the qualifications required by the ISA."

Sounded legit. Now all she had to do was make a quick exit and get on with the planning. She zipped up her down jacket.

"No one outside of Red River," said Councilman Flaps.

Councilwoman Maureen nodded. "We agreed to this as long as our own residents were put in key positions. This is Red River. We look out for our own."

Right.

The heat of anger flickered to life in Sandra's chest and spiraled out until her fingertips burned.

Not a lot of people had come to her defense when she was a frightened teen who had been lucky to get off with community service, a mandatory twelve step program, and probation that required random drug tests. All for a crime she hadn't committed.

The familiar sting of humiliation bit at her gut, just as it had every time she'd had to stand up and say *I'm Sandra, and I'm a recovering addict* in front of a room full of strangers. What she'd really wanted to yell was *my dad stole the pills and let me take the fall for it! I was just working at the pharmacy after school to spend time with him.*

She held up a palm. "I understand your concerns, but there isn't another Red River resident available who meets the criteria. Taos is our neighbor, and their local businesses stand to gain from this event, too, so I'm sure I'll be able to find a few qualified people to pick from." It was a win-win as far as she was concerned.

She adjusted her shimmery lavender knit hat and flipped the matching scarf over one shoulder to cover her neck.

Councilman Cowboy Hat let out a sound that was close to a grunt. "Businesses in Taos are also our biggest competition, and I don't trust outsiders when Red River has so much to lose. All it takes is one bad review on a travel site to ruin our reputation." He waggled an index finger. "One reviewer trash talking us could do a lot of damage."

Sandra let her eyelids fall shut and spring open several times, blinking away the disbelief.

Did they remember who they were talking to?

For years, she'd been pinned with the blame every time merchandise went missing from one of the stores along Main Street. Denying it did no good because no one believed a drug addict. Or someone who'd pretended to be one.

"I'm aware." She reached for the chairback sitting next to her and white-knuckled it.

"How about Doc Holloway?" Councilwoman Maureen asked.

Sandra stepped forward to gather up her notes. "Blake Holloway is our only local medical doctor, so he's in charge of the aid station we're setting up at the base of the lifts. The safety officer has to be on skis patrolling the slopes, and Doc Holloway can't be in two places at once," she said, scooping up her notepad to leave before a council member brought up the one organization in Red River she didn't want to consider. The one *person* in town she had to avoid at all costs, for his own good.

She took a step backward toward the door, the old wood planks creaking under her flat all-weather boots. "We have no choice but to look for a replacement outside of Red River, and Taos is the next best place to find someone qualified. I'll let you know the second I have a few good candidates." She took another step backward. A few more steps and she'd be able to turn and dash for the door. "If you'd prefer, the council can even interview them and make the final decision."

"The Red River fire department!" blurted Chairperson Clydelle.

Sandra's heart dropped to her feet, and her chest deflated.

Of course, Clydelle wouldn't miss an opportunity to see the local firefighters in action. Before she became the council chair, she spent so much time trying to get any...or all of them to take off their shirts, she should've been sued for sexual harassment.

Sandra clutched her notes to her chest and glanced over a shoulder at the exit.

So close.

"I considered that." *Liar, liar.* Her insulated leggings might as well go up in flames. "The entire fire department will be on call during the competition in case of emergencies." She'd called the fire chief in advance and made sure the Person Who Would Never Be Named Publicly...to preserve his own reputation...would be busy doing something far away from her. She waved her hand in the air dismissively. "I've got this handled." A few peanut shells crunched under her feet as she took another step back. "I'll find a trustworthy replacement, even if they're not from Red River."

The council members frowned at her like anyone not from Red River might as well be from Mars.

Sandra resisted the urge to pinch the bridge of her nose by stuffing her free hand into the pocket of her purple down jacket. "You all are worried about Red River's rep. That's understandable." Not to mention it was the council's job. "If we don't fill the safety officer's position immediately, we'll be at risk of the ISA canceling the event all together. They've already had to move it once, remember? That's how we were able to bring it here. Think of the damage *that* will do to us on travel sites. People from all over the world have booked rooms and paid for travel expenses to get here. It seems, to me, finding a replacement outside of Red River is much less risky than losing the event all together."

Chairperson Clydelle took another sip, then cradled the cup with both hands, leaving a ring of creamer on her upper lip. "You're right, dear. Which is why I've taken the liberty of inviting the only person left in Red River who is perfect for the position."

Worry prickled up Sandra's spine.

Joe's door swung open behind her, a rush of freezing cold air blustering in to chill the cavernous room.

A shiver rushed over her. She did not want to turn around. She didn't.

Unfortunately, she didn't have to.

Langston Brooks, all six feet two of hard alpha male and the person she was trying to avoid, stepped up beside her. "Morning."

Her skin burned as his gaze licked over her. And she was covered head to toe in winter gear!

When she refused to meet his stare, or even return his greeting, he turned his attention to the council. "You asked to see me, Ms. Clydelle?"

"Mmm hmmm." The chairperson's voice turned to a coo, and she batted her eyelashes as though she were watching a Magic Mike show live in Vegas.

Oh, good grief.

"We're wasting valuable time." Sandra glanced at her watch, only to realize she wasn't wearing one. Involuntarily, her eyes flitted up to meet Langston's, and her heart skipped a beat.

Laughter shimmered in his dark soulful eyes. The lights glinted off his wavy chestnut hair.

God, she loved those eyes. And that hair.

"I..." Her voice went croaky. She swallowed back the cotton in her mouth. "I—"

"Langston, dear, how would you like to be the new safety officer for the snowboarding championship?" Clydelle batted her eyes several more times.

Sandra's throat closed.

No. Just no. "I don't think that's a good idea—"

"I'd love to be considered," said Langston, smiling at her like a cat who'd just eaten an entire pet shop full of canaries.

Sandra pulled her stare from his squared jaw. From his mocha eyes. From his delicious looking mouth.

Heat curled through her, settling in places it shouldn't.

Dammit.

"I just need a little time to find someone—"

Clydelle lifted a boney finger, silencing Sandra. Then she lifted her mug to signal Dylan McCoy, who was behind the long bar, lining up fresh glasses. He wasn't in line to take over Cotton Eyed Joe's soon for no reason. The guy had superpowers behind the bar and read every customer like a well-worn book, delivering refills before Clydelle lowered that finger.

The scent of fresh warm coffee, cinnamon, and liqueur settled over them. Sandra wasn't much of a drinker, but on a snowy late February morning...in front of what felt like a hit squad...she could use a mug of hot spiced rum. Heavy on the rum, please.

As if Dylan could read her mind, he finished passing out mugs to the council, then pressed one into Langston's hand, then Sandra's. "Tough crowd this morning. Good luck." Dylan smiled and winked at her. His hip musician look was even cuter than usual when dimples appeared. "Alcohol free." He nodded at her cup.

Sandra sighed. She'd never shake the addict reputation in this little town. It refused to go away, constantly prickling over her like a bad skin condition.

Never mind that she'd been the one to perpetuate it as a cover.

Involuntarily, she glanced at Langston. As usual, his formidable stature held an air of confidence that commanded respect. Respect that she'd never have if she stayed in Red River.

Respect that she'd never wanted him to lose because of her.

She stared into her mug as the council started to chatter amongst themselves, as though they'd forgotten she was there. A ribbon of steam unfurled under her nose, and she breathed it in to settle her buzzing nerves. It smelled divine. She took a sip and let the warm liquid slide down her throat.

Too bad it *didn't* contain alcohol. A little liquid courage never hurt a gal who was fighting for her future. Especially when the gal wasn't exactly the town sweetheart.

"Sandra, why am I the only person in town you haven't asked to help with this event?" Langston said low enough for only her to hear, then sipped at his coffee.

Her stomach churned, as if one of the blizzards that turned Red River into a winter wonderland every year had taken up residence in her gut. "You know why." She kept her tone low, too. Chairperson Clydelle was old, and the council was preoccupied with a discussion about the Chamber of Commerce building needing new gutters before the spring melt started, but her hearing had satellite capabilities when she wanted to scoop the latest gossip.

"Actually, I don't." Langston rolled the coffee around in his mug before taking another drink. "I'm the best person for the job, and you know it."

Yes, she did know. But she was very close to finally making her escape from a town that would never fully forgive her for the past. Even after years of saving a down payment so she could buy the failing ski shop, where she'd worked since high school, then turning it around so it made a profit, a cloud of suspicion still followed her. Once the people of Red River were crossed, it was hard to earn their trust again.

Which was why the council hadn't been too eager to approve hosting the competition since it was her idea. It was also the reason they were being difficult now. They didn't completely trust her judgment, even though the ISA had hired her as the local event coordinator.

With the payday she'd get, plus the extra revenue that was sure to flow into her ski shop that winter because of the international news coverage, she'd pay off the shop's mortgage and shut it down since she hadn't been able to find a buyer. Then she'd be free to move on to greener pastures. Pastures where no one knew of her past and couldn't hold it against her anymore.

She shifted from one foot to the other. "We can't work closely together. It's over, Langston," she whispered.

The backs of her eyes stung. She needed to get out of there before she made an ass of herself. Before she let the growing storm of emotions she'd been holding back flow like a rushing river. Before she caved and threw herself into his arms.

She cleared her throat. "Excuse me." She raised her voice to get the council's attention.

Their chatter didn't subside in the least.

"Have it your way, Sans." Langston chuckled under his breath.

The tension between Sandra's shoulders subsided. *Whew.*

Finally, he was going to be reasonable about their...their...*ack!* She didn't even know what to call it.

"Madam Chairperson," he said several decibels louder than normal.

The council quieted, and Clydelle batted eyelashes at Langston once more.

Sandra's eyes rolled so far back in her head her vision blurred.

Well, at least Langston was going to help stop this nonsense once and for all, and now she could get on with finding a replacement.

"I'm grateful for the council's consideration." He lifted his mug.

Sandra waited for Langston's "but." That one beautiful little word that would close the meeting so she could get back to work. Thank *gawd.*

"I humbly accept the position as safety officer for the extreme snowboarding championship, if you'll entrust it to me."

What? Sandra's head whiplashed toward Langston.

Speechless, she glared at him.

He took a long drink of coffee from his mug, winking at her over the rim.

"No!" Her eyes slid shut for a beat. "No," she said again, trying to sound calm. Unfortunately, her heart thundered against her chest so loud the next county probably heard it. "I mean, Mr. Brooks..."

One of his silky brows arched high in that sexy way, which usually had her sighing like a high school girl with a crush.

She tried to ignore it. Really, she did.

Her uterus still did a dance.

"Mr. Brooks already has a critical job that may be needed during the event." Sandra's words tumbled out all at once. "What if someone gets lost in the wilderness? What if someone gets hurt so badly, they need to be lifted out by helicopter? Mr. Brooks is the best flight medic in northern New Mexico *and* southern

Colorado." She couldn't work with him. Not when she was so close to finally escaping her past.

"I can easily line up another flight medic to cover my shifts during the event," he said to the council, as though she wasn't standing right there. "I've covered for several people in both states. They'll do the same for me."

"Then our fire department might need him," she blurted. "Lang...I mean, *Mr. Brooks* still works as a paramedic here in Red River when they need him, and when he's not on call for a helo flight." Something she probably shouldn't readily admit to knowing. Their past relationship, which she'd insisted be publicly acknowledged as nothing more than a few one-night stands, could hurt *his* reputation if it ever came to light. Plus, she was rambling. "And with so many tourists in town..." She sputtered with laughter to turn the tide back in her favor. "...and *hello,* so many extreme snowboarders barreling down the slopes, we're likely to need a lot of paramedics. Look what happened to Coop just last night."

So much rambling.

The cup in Sandra's hand shook, and the brown liquid sloshed over the side.

Jeez.

"I move to name Langston Brooks as the event's new safety officer," said Councilwoman Maureen, as though she hadn't heard a word Sandra said.

"I second the motion," said Councilman Flaps.

Chairperson Clydelle banged her pen against the scarred table. "It's official. We're adjourned!"

Chairs scrapped against the floor as the council stood and gathered up their coats and belongings without actually putting the motion to a final vote.

Seriously?

Stunned, Sandra's mouth fell open. She'd called the meeting as a courtesy to keep the peace with the council. The final decision didn't actually need the council's approval. "What the heck just happened?" Wait. Had she said that out loud?

Langston shifted his large frame, closing the space between them. "I think I just became an important part of your event staff."

Dammit. She *had* said it out loud.

She spun to face him, steam practically billowing from her ears. "Why did you do that? You undermined my authority, not to mention the fact that you *know* this is a bad idea." Her head snapped around to make sure no one was listening. Thank goodness the council was already filtering toward the door. "You know how people in this town are. If we spend a lot of time together, which we will with you as the safety officer, they'll start talking."

"So let them talk." He shrugged.

So angry she was at a loss for words, she simply let out a frustrated huff.

Langston stared at his mug, the muscle in his jaw ticking. Finally, he said, "Hell, Sans. If you don't want people to talk about us, then maybe we shouldn't have been sleeping together the past ten years."

Twelve years. If the two years of hot and heavy making out in high school counted.

"That's over, remember?" How could he not? She'd told him to his face so he could finally move on without her dragging him down like an anchor sinking a ship.

Langston leaned closer. "If it makes you feel better, then keep telling yourself that." He placed his mug on the table. "But you and I both know it's never going to be over between us." He turned to leave but hesitated. "*Mr. Brooks?* Really, Sans? I know you've always wanted to keep our relationship a secret, but calling me Mr. Brooks when I've seen you naked..." His gaze slid down her length. Even though she was clothed in full winter gear, his eyes darkened as if he was picturing her with nothing on at all.

Her skin prickled, and the room suddenly grew warm. Heat slid through her, settling between her thighs. She clenched every muscle from the waist down.

"Yes, well..." She hugged her papers to her chest. "It was fun, but it's time to move on. This will be nothing more than work between us." She smiled, realizing she did have a card to play. "And as far as the snowboarding event is concerned, I'm your boss."

A slow, naughty smile spread across his face. "That makes it all the more interesting." He strolled through the front door, leaving Sandra staring after him.

Leaving her more determined than ever to keep their working relationship purely professional.

Leaving her wanting him more than ever.

CHAPTER TWO

The second the door to Cotton Eyed Joe's closed at Langston's back and the frigid February air engulfed him, he dropped his cool *I'm an alpha dude who's always in control of my emotions* act and clenched his gloved hands into fists.

How could Sandra let him go so easily? He'd gone along with her ridiculous plan to keep their relationship a secret for years. And don't get him started on her obnoxious flirtations with every eligible guy in town just so the locals wouldn't get suspicious and figure out she and Langston had been a couple for a decade.

He'd had to restrain himself more than once from teaching intoxicated male patrons at Joe's some manners when they'd gotten into Sandra's personal space. Taken the liberty of stroking her long, silky, caramel colored hair. Let their eyes settle too long on her gorgeous rack, with cleavage as deep as the Grand Canyon. Even though Langston knew she was putting on a show to hide their relationship, he'd still wanted to take a few guys out back and show them who their daddy was.

Instead, he'd waited patiently for her to finally come to her senses and either tell the truth about her father or stop caring what people thought.

Langston sure as hell didn't care. As far as he was concerned,

Sandra came first. Everyone else could either get on board with their relationship or piss off. Still, she insisted on keeping their affair a closely guarded secret, afraid he'd lose his friends and family if the truth came out. The more he pushed to out themselves, the more Sandra backed away from him.

Until he'd finally insisted that she make an honest man out of him. At which point she'd refused the black velvet box that housed the gigantic diamond rock he'd tried to give her. Then she broke up with him.

Obviously, he didn't get women.

But he knew someone who did, and he desperately needed some advice.

He jammed both fisted hands into the pockets of his gray down coat and trudged along the nicely shoveled sidewalks of Main Street toward his parents' real estate office. His sister, Lorenda, had gone back to school to finish her degree in music education, but still showed houses when she wasn't attending classes. During the winter, real estate moved slow in a small vacation town like Red River, so Lorenda spent most of her time in the office studying, and their parents spent most of their time traveling like the semi-retired folks they were.

The fact that Langston was about to ask his sister to help figure out his love life wasn't something he was proud of, especially since he was still carrying the damn ring box in his pocket, even after Sandra had rejected his proposal. He was even less proud of sneaking around and pretending not to care about Sandra. They were grown ass adults, and he was tired of hiding.

He lengthened his strides.

A man's gotta do what a man's gotta do.

At the intersection, he stepped off the curb onto the icy street.

And sank into the banked snow up to the middle of his calves.

Cold slush poured over the tops of his winter boots, soaking his insulated socks.

He let the frigid air fill his hollow chest.

Life couldn't suck any worse at a time in his life when he

should be enjoying it to the fullest. He'd paid his dues. Built a great career he loved. Waited patiently for the woman he wanted.

Yet here he was—standing in a crossroads, alone, wet, and cold as hell.

For the first few years, sneaking around with Sandra had been fun. Exciting. Eventually, though, hiding got old and tiring. Especially as his friends and sister found their soulmates, one by one.

Which was why he needed advice.

He crossed the intersection, feet squishing in his boots, and sidestepped an icy patch in the center of the road. He veered left toward the Red River Police Department SUV that was parked along the curb in front of Brooks Real Estate.

Score.

That meant his buddy since high school, who was now his brother-in-law and Red River's newest deputy, was there, too, and Langston could use another guy's perspective. He'd get a two-fer, and he trusted no one more than Lorenda and Mitchell.

The way Langston saw it, he had two choices. Keep trying to convince Sandra that their relationship didn't depend on anyone else other than themselves. Not family, not friends, and certainly not town gossip over something that happened well over a decade ago. And even though everyone in town still thought Sandra was guilty, it shouldn't matter. She'd paid her debt to society, and she deserved to move past it. Or walk away and give Sandra what she said she wanted—to be left alone.

He'd waited a long time for her, but maybe she was right. Maybe their time together was over. Maybe he should start dating other women. Try to find someone who wanted to settle down. Hell, at this point, he'd be happy with someone who'd just hold his hand in public instead of pretending they barely knew each other except in the occasional biblical sense.

Problem was there was no other woman for him. Only Sandra.

A bell jingled as Langston stepped inside and pushed the door closed to keep out the winter cold.

The front office was empty.

He stomped snow off his feet on the mat and pulled off his thick, insulated gloves. "Hello?" he called out. His sister and no-account husband—who Langston loved like a brother but had to constantly razz because razzing was number one in the Man Rules...plus, it was fun as hell—could've walked to one of the diners for breakfast.

The door was unlocked, but that didn't mean much. Crime had always been low in Red River, but had dropped to as close to zero as possible once Mitchell joined the police department.

Langston reached inside his coat, retrieved his phone, and called Lorenda. A phone went off from the depths of the back offices, and his call went directly to voicemail. A text message dinged, and he looked at the screen.

In the middle of something, I'll call you back.

Huh. What could be so important during Brooks Real Estate's slow season that his sister wouldn't come out of the back offices to say a quick hello?

Langston dialed Mitchell's number.

Another phone blared to life from somewhere in the back offices, and Langston's head snapped up.

Ah, hell. Obviously, Mitchell was in the middle of the same *something* as Lorenda.

Langston turned to leave, but then he stopped short. As much as he didn't want to picture his sister *in the middle of something,* she was with her husband. In broad daylight, at work, without locking the door. Because that's what married folks could do.

That's what Langston wanted. And he wanted it with Sandra.

He jerked the door open and the bell jingled to life again.

A door to the back office opened, and Langston glanced over a shoulder to see his brother-in-law's head jutting through the small crack.

His hair was tousled, and his khaki deputy's shirt was all messed up. "What's up, buddy? Anything wrong?" He kept his voice casual, as though he hadn't just been interrupted in the middle of...*something*.

"Nothing wrong." Not true, but that was about to change.

"Did you need something?" asked Mitchell.

"Not anymore." Langston had just figured out the answer himself. He waved off Mitchell. "Go back to what you were doing. Sorry I, uh, interrupted."

Mitchell gave him an innocent look. Which told Langston that his buddy was guilty as hell.

"Who says I was doing anything that couldn't be interrupted?"

Langston smirked, pointing to Mitchell's shirt. "Your shirt buttons aren't lined up right."

Mitchell looked down at his misaligned shirt, and his eyes flew wide.

"I'll catch up with you later, dude." Langston flipped the lock on the inside doorknob to give his sister and brother-in-law some privacy, and stepped out into the cold again to go talk some long overdue sense into his woman.

She was stuck with him until the snowboarding championship was over, and he wasn't giving up until she listened to reason.

But first, he had to make a couple of stops to gather the ammo he'd need when he confronted Sandra. He would run by his house a few blocks off Main Street to get Zeus because she couldn't resist that dog's big droopy eyes and loveable personality. Then Langston would stop by the Ostergaard's German bakery. Mrs. O's cranberry pecan scones were Sandra's favorite treat. A secret weapon, and he wasn't going to bring a knife to a gun fight. He was bringing something much more powerful. Pastries.

He smiled to himself and headed down the street toward his house.

He was in the fight of his life. A life that wouldn't be complete without Sans.

So he wasn't above fighting dirty.

CHAPTER THREE

Sandra was going to stroke out if she didn't calm the earthquake of panic rocking her insides.

The flash flood of heated attraction that still hadn't receded after seeing Langston at the council meeting didn't help either. Since high school, it had been that way between them.

At the rear of her shop—*Up To Snow Good, Winter Sports and More*—she racked a snowboard and started sanding the nicked up edges for a customer who was scheduled to pick it up soon. When she was done, she waxed it to a fine shine.

"Who does Langston Brooks think he is?" she mumbled to herself, picking up the diamond sanding block. Absently, she worked on the edges of the board again, gaining speed with each swipe.

Who was she kidding?

Langston knew exactly who he was, and so did everyone else in Red River.

Town hotshot. Town hero. Town hottie.

A confident man who was fearless, selfless, and desirable as hell.

Which was why she'd vowed to avoid him when she'd rejected

his absurd marriage proposal and broken things off for good. The pull was too strong. The chemistry was too intense.

The cost was too high.

Her life had been hard enough, filled with so much regret. She couldn't bear more if his family and friends turned on him because of her. Or if he lost the respect he'd earned from saving countless lives and thinking of others before he thought of himself. Always.

So she'd done him the favor—not that he would call it that—of thinking of him first by turning him down and ending their relationship. Even though what she'd really wanted to do was scream *YES!* from the rooftops for everyone to hear. Then she'd wanted to jump into his arms, wrap her arms around his neck and her legs around his lean waist, and kiss the stuffing out of him.

Dear Lord, how was she going to get through this event with him filling one of the most important jobs? Working closely with her every day, as she'd been doing with the event staff from day one.

Swipe, swipe, swipe.

A bead of perspiration rose across her forehead as she took out her annoyance on the board.

"You're gonna file it into a sewing needle if you don't stop." The rich timbre of Langston's voice slid through her like fine wine.

She whirled, stumbling back into a round sale rack of winter snowsuits. Before she could fully recover her balance, Langston's Great Dane, Zeus, bounded in her direction. Zeus adored her. Unfortunately, he also adored rough housing with her, as though he were the size of a Chihuahua. She hadn't seen him since the breakup. In his excitement, he reared up and put his front paws against her shoulders, knocking her backwards.

"Zeus!" Langston scolded.

Did no good.

Sandra disappeared through the hanging snowsuits, falling to the floor under the rack.

The front half of Zeus' body appeared through the sale merchandise, and he licked her face with his gigantic tongue.

"Good to see you, too, big guy." Sandra stroked his black and white spotted coat.

She could lay there in the dark under the clothing rack until Langston left. That would be preferable to having to resist his smile and ridiculous good looks.

"Um." A part appeared between a pair of lady's leopard print ski pants and a lime green parka. "You okay, Sans?" He held a white paper bag in one hand. The aroma was divine, and Sandra knew what was inside. Only Langston would bring her favorite pastry.

She let her head fall back for a beat. "Fine." She pushed herself up, ignoring his outstretched hand, and climbed from under the rack of clothing. She used her sleeve to wipe Zeus' kisses from her cheek. "Just a little wet."

Langston's gaze went sultry, and an awkward silence filled the room.

God, she loved it when he looked at her that way. As though she was the only woman in the whole world who could capture his attention. As though he wanted her and only her. Right then. Right there.

She smoothed a hand over her hair, which she'd pulled back into a ponytail so she could work on the board. "You highjacked my meeting and my event."

"It needed to be highjacked because you weren't thinking of what's best for the safety officer's job." He reached for a stray lock that had escaped the ponytail.

She leaned away, and he let his hand drop to his side.

If she felt his warm, tender touch, her resolve would crumble. "So now you don't have any more faith in me than the rest of this town?" A hand went to her hip.

His gaze followed, then trailed upward. Heat licked over her as he let those gorgeous, dark eyes linger on the skin where her fleece pullover opened at the neck. Slowly, they climbed to her mouth and stayed there even longer.

Finally, he said, "Oh, I have faith in you." He pretended to tap knuckles against the side of her head. "I know the intelligence in that hard, little head of yours. Which is the reason I don't get why you never would let our relationship go public. And I certainly can't understand why you won't give up this laughable notion that it's over between us."

Because I don't want you to have to choose between me and everyone... everything you care about.

What kind of person would put someone they loved in such an impossible position?

Her breath hitched.

Love.

She swallowed hard, forcing air back into her lungs.

She did still love Langston. But she could never tell him so again. If she did, he'd never give up on her. And he really, really needed to give up on her, even if he didn't realize it yet.

"Fine." She marched to the front counter, pulled out two specific pieces of paper from a file folder, and marched right back to Langston. "Here."

He held out his free hand, the white paper bag still in the other.

Ignoring the pull of warm pastry aroma, she shoved the papers at him. "The top sheet is a list of the safety officer's responsibilities for the event." The ISA had sent her a job description for each required position so she could hire people with the right skill sets. "The bottom sheet is a list of the entire event staff, along with our cell numbers and emails. We're meeting daily since it's only a few weeks away."

"I'll be ready." He glanced around the store, taking everything in for the first time since he'd arrived. He hadn't been to her shop since they'd broken up, and a crease appeared between his brows. "Why do you have so much stuff on sale? You don't usually run sales on your winter gear until your summer merchandise is about to arrive, and it's way too early in the year for that."

Shee-ot. She didn't want him to know that she was trying to get rid of as much merchandise as possible before she closed the shop and left town. She'd already informed the landlord that she wouldn't be renewing her lease. With the extra shoppers the snowboarding championship would bring in, she could reduce her inventory substantially and close up shop as soon as the ski and snowboarding season started winding down.

If Langston found out about her plan, he'd throw up every obstacle he could to stop her from leaving.

She raised a shoulder but glanced away, unable to look him in the eye. "Just getting rid of some overstocked items."

A tremor of guilt rocketed through her. Well, it wasn't a lie. Not really.

He raised the white paper bag in his hand. "Brought you something."

Her mouth watered. "I'm not hungry."

"You've never needed to be hungry to enjoy your favorite scone from the Ostergaard's bakery." He kept holding out the bag.

"Langston," she whispered, her voice a little desperate. A little helpless against both the scone and his gesture because she knew what would come next. They'd done that dance a thousand times. He'd feed her one morsel, as though it was foreplay. She'd moan and open her mouth so he could place another bite on her tongue. By the time the scone was gone, they'd both be so aroused they'd end up naked against the storage room wall. "Don't do this to yourself."

Ha! She doubted he was suffering even half as much as her.

He sat the papers on top of a rack, opened the pastry sack, and withdrew a small piece of scone. Then he stepped into her space and held it to her lips, like he'd done so many times before. It was their special ritual after he'd been away for several days, working helo life flights.

She should smack his hand away. She should.

Instead, her lips parted, and he placed the morsel on her tongue.

It literally melted in her mouth, her taste buds bursting at the flavor.

She moaned, her eyes sliding shut.

A deep, guttural groan escaped from him, too, and he molded a palm to her neck, his fingertips sending desire bolting through her.

He nipped a crumb from her bottom lip, and yep, her resistance disintegrated into dust.

When her lips parted, his tongue swiped across hers. Once, twice.

Her arms laced around his neck, one set of fingers disappearing into his hair, and the gentle caresses of his tongue against hers turned ravenous as he devoured her mouth with a punishing kiss.

The bag fell to the floor as his solid arms closed around her, molding her body to his. Even through his winter coat, his heat enveloped her. Always did.

Always would unless she stopped this nonsense.

He must've sensed her momentary return to sanity, because one large hand found her ass cheek and he pulled her tighter.

A jingle of the bell as the front door to the shop opened had her breaking away from him, and instantly she missed his touch.

"Hey," said the snowboarder who'd stopped into the shop earlier. She was mid-twenties and dressed head to toe in white snow gear, a sign of her expertise on the slopes. Only an experienced snowboarder who knew they wouldn't be falling a lot would wear white. "I'm here to pick up my board. Beautiful dog." She smiled, staring at Zeus. "Bon appétit, dude."

Sandra looked down, taking in the mess at her feet.

The paper bag from the bakery was torn to shreds. Crumbs dotted the commercial grade carpet.

Zeus' downcast puppy dog eyes telegraphed his guilt. Then he let out a small belch.

"Looks like he's been a naughty boy," the snowboarder said. She gave Zeus a wink. "My kind of guy."

Sandra's stare locked with Langston's. Like father like dog. The smoky look in his eyes said he wanted to get naughty.

She wanted that, too, more than she could ever admit.

The snowboarder cleared her throat. "Um, how much do I owe you?"

Sandra pried her gaze from Langston's, hurried to the board, and handed it over. "I'll meet you at the front register in a sec."

When she and Langston were alone again at the back of the store, she said, "I've got work to do." She retrieved the papers from the top of the clothing rack and handed them to Langston. "Don't forget these."

"I'll look over these and call you with questions." He took the papers. "Better yet, I'll stop by to ask questions in person." One corner of his delicious looking mouth quirked up. "I'm looking forward to working with you, Sans. Every day we spend together will only prove that I'm right."

Her pulse quickened. "I'm the boss, and I'm telling you don't stop by. Besides having a business to run, coordinating this event keeps me insanely busy. I'll only have time to see you at the daily staff meetings." She headed toward the cash register, but then stopped and angled her body back toward him again. "Don't call either, unless you have a real question." She nodded to the typed job description in his hand. "Which means I don't expect to hear from you at all outside of the staff meetings because, as you claimed in the council meeting this morning, you can do the job in your sleep." She'd just driven her point home, so he'd know calling her with silly questions just to talk to her wouldn't be well received. "With both hands tied and possibly even blindfolded."

Instead of looking contrite, Langston looked...amused. At her!

He stepped into her space again, glancing over her shoulder, as though he was making sure they weren't being watched by the customer who waited at the front register.

Well, at least he could still be discreet.

"Oh, I'm going to get the job done." His voice turned husky, and laughter sparkled in his eyes. "But you'll be the one tied up and possibly even blindfolded." He leaned in and whispered, "And there won't be any sleeping going on...*boss.*"

Heat prickled over her.

Enough was enough. She had to end this.

"I've told you it's over." Her heart thudded against her ribcage at what she was about to say. It was awful. *She* was awful. But it had to be done. If Langston refused to look out for himself, then she had to do it for him. That's what love was—putting someone else before yourself.

Right?

She hauled in a breath. "I don't love you anymore, Langston. That's why I ended our affair. That's why you need to forget about me."

Tears stung the backs of her eyes, and she could hardly breathe. *So this is what a broken heart feels like?* She'd experienced it after her father threw her under the bus when she was still just a teenager. But this? *This* was much, much worse.

Langston pulled winter gloves from his pocket and turned them over in his hands. "Right, about you ending our affair." He stared at his gloves as they tumbled over and over in his hands. "I called bullshit then, and I call bullshit now."

He brushed passed her and let out a sharp whistle. Zeus gave her a sad look, then fell in line behind Langston.

For the second time that day, he left her speechless. Flustered. And not feeling the least bit like a boss.

CHAPTER FOUR

Langston leaned against the back wall in the main lodge at the base of the slopes, arms folded over his chest and legs crossed at the ankles.

It was day five since his addition to the event staff, and as the safety officer, he waited for his turn to give an update. The *boss* usually made him go last.

The room full of staff chomped on donuts from the Ostergaard's bakery, courtesy of Sandra.

Smart.

Free food or booze usually increased attendance at just about any gathering, and she had provided fresh, warm pastries at every daily staff meeting.

Holding a clipboard and looking hot as hell in a pair of black leggings, faux fur lined boots that hit her mid-calf, and a black turtleneck sweater—all of which fit her like a body glove—she listened patiently. Every person in charge of a task took a turn. With a red pen, Sandra ticked off items on her clipboard and made notes.

The lady in charge of concessions finished up her report about how the order of extra hot chocolate, marshmallows, and paper cups needed to accommodate the mammoth sized crowd they were expecting for the event was driving her insane. Ordering from different suppliers because the regular wholesale food vendor for the lodge couldn't fill the entire order was, apparently, very stressful. The woman seemed worried the crowd might riot if they ran out of cocoa.

Langston covered a yawn with his hand, which drew a scowl from his boss.

Hell, if he'd known that was all it would take to get Sandra to acknowledge him, he'd have yawned the second he walked into the meeting. She'd spent every day ignoring him as though he didn't exist. Since she'd told him she didn't love him anymore, the only time she'd looked *at* him instead of *through* him was when it was his turn to give the safety officer's daily progress report.

So instead of just yawning, Langston gave her an innocent look and stretched, as if he'd rather be home in bed. Truth was he *would* rather be home in bed, as long as Sandra's naked body was tangled with his.

Her scowl deepened to a full-on glare.

He refolded his arms and went back to holding up the wall.

Talmadge Oaks, another high school buddy and world-renowned green architect who'd returned to Red River a while back and married a gorgeous local innkeeper—gave an update on the construction of the course for the competition, per the International Snowboarding Association's guidelines. It had just been finished the day before, and the ISA was sending a representative out to look at it before giving their stamp of approval.

Next, Clifford—Red River's most popular maintenance man—started his hand-wringing spiel over whether or not the number of portable outhouses should be increased. Same concern he'd voiced during every damn meeting.

The man did have a point, though. Langston would give him that. The event was going to draw an enormous amount of people from far and wide. A shortage of toilets could get ugly.

"We've been over this with the vendor," Sandra assured Clifford. "They know how many people we're expecting and have sent more than enough units."

Clifford plopped back into his seat, still wringing his hands.

Poor guy.

The world needed guys like Clifford because his job was a dirty one, and someone had to do it.

Finally, it was Langston's turn. He pushed off the wall. "Since the course is finished, I'll need to take a look at it."

Sandra nodded, her expression unreadable.

"When we're done here, I'll go up the lifts and ski down to check the spectator barriers." It was his job to assess risk, and no one was getting hurt on his watch.

"Can I go with you?" A member of the ski patrol, Jordyn, beamed at him.

As safety officer, the ski patrol for the event reported to him. Directing them was one of the responsibilities listed on the ISA's job description that Sandra had printed and given to him. Most of the members were already part of Red River's regular winter season ski patrol who helped out injured skiers on the slopes, but a few new faces had shown up from different parts of the state. One of them was this particularly cute blonde with a personality as bouncy as her curly hair. She was a first-year nursing student and had been looking at Langston with adoration from the moment she found out he was a flight medic.

Something flared in Sandra's eyes.

Huh.

Jordyn inched closer.

Which seemed to cause Sandra's eyes to narrow into slits.

Well, well, well.

He'd been waiting for an opening to call out Sandra's indifference as the bullshit that it was. This might just be the chance he'd been waiting for.

Unfortunately, he'd have to pull a dick move and flirt with a girl who was already crushing on him. He glanced at the innocence in Jordyn's bright blue eyes. The kid couldn't be more than nineteen.

Was being labeled a dickhead worth chipping away at Sandra's *I don't love you anymore* lie?

Jordyn's smile widened, and she eased even closer so their arms brushed.

If Sandra's eyes could shoot daggers, Langston would be ducking for cover.

Totally worth being a dickhead. Frankly, he'd been called worse.

But hell no. He couldn't bring himself to lead on someone he had zero interest in. Plus, impressionable nineteen-year-old girls weren't his style. He wanted a real woman who could challenge him. Keep him in line. Kick his ass when he needed it. Which was far too often if he had to be honest.

He kept his gaze trained on Sandra. "I could use the company out there on the slopes. Haven't had much lately." He let a beat go by without breaking eye contact with her, waiting for her to rise to the challenge.

She said nothing.

"I'll go!" No joke, Jordyn bounced on the balls of her feet, and Langston half expected her to raise her hand like they were in high school.

Fuck's sake.

"I can always use more time on the slopes," Jordyn said with the enthusiasm of a high school cheerleader at a championship game.

Nice as she was, he was *not* going out onto the slopes alone with a teenie bopper.

Two tables were occupied with the rest of the ski patrol crew. They weren't hard to pick out of a crowd. Seeing as how their jobs were out on the slopes, they were already dressed in ski gear and matching red winter coats that had *Ski Patrol* printed in bright yellow letters across the backs. He found Calvin Wells, Cooper Wells' much younger brother, in the crowd. He was a good-looking kid with even better manners, and he was much closer to Jordyn's age than Langston.

He went over and whispered in Cal's ear, "You'll join us." It wasn't a request, it was a command.

"Yes, sir," Cal said.

Which made Langston feel a million years old.

Sandra pulled on a black down coat, covered her ears with a faux fur headband that matched her boots, and said, "Meeting adjourned. I need to look at the barriers, too, so I'll go with Langston and..." Her gaze shifted to Jordyn, as though Sandra was trying to remember her name.

"Jordyn!" Her blonde curls bounced as she all but shouted her own name.

"Jordyn," Sandra said slowly with an eyeroll in her voice.

Jordyn clapped and bounced. "That's me!"

Dear Lord.

Well, at least his plan had actually worked, and Sandra was coming. Just not *coming* in the way he'd like. He chuckled to himself. It had been far too long since that had happened, and he planned to remedy that as soon as possible.

Outside, Sandra snapped on both skis, secured a pole around each wrist and stabbed them into the fresh powder. "Ready?"

"Ready!" Jordyn said.

Jeez. Sandra was glad her eyes were covered with polarized sunglasses to hide her eye roll.

"I'm ready," Cal said.

Thank goodness he was going with them, so she wouldn't have to focus on Jordyn's constant hero worship for Langston. By the second day he'd joined the staff and started attending the daily meetings, her doe-eyed fawning over him had started to make Sandra nauseous.

Okay, so he *was* a hero. And incredibly good-looking.

Still...

"You're going to ski without ski pants?" Langston pulled on his gloves.

"My leggings are made for weather like this." Not completely true, but not a total lie either. They were made for extreme temperatures, but were supposed to be worn under snow pants. Sandra wasn't about to wuss out, though. Not with a pretty young woman, who still had a body that hadn't yet experienced gravity, giving Langston googly eyes.

One of his silky brows arched high. A move that was usually his way of saying *bullshit*.

She ignored it. "We won't be out that long," she said. "I've seen millennials snowboard in nothing but a helmet just to get a laugh from friends." Until Deputy Sheriff Mitchell Langston hauled them away in cuffs when they reached the bottom of the run. "I'll be fine." Darned right she would. She could still do anything a sprightly nineteen-year-old could do.

"Whatever you say. Let's go." He placed the sporty sunglasses hanging around his neck onto the bridge of his nose. The shades made him even more drop dead gorgeous in a badass kind of way.

Jordyn sighed. Out loud.

Oh, good grief.

Sandra pushed off, heading to the main lift.

"Hold up," Langston said.

She fishtailed her skis to one side, coming to a stop.

Langston skied up beside her. "We need to go up the other lift."

"Why?" she asked. "This one's closer to the course."

"We can get a better look at the spectator barriers from the other lift. This one has a copse of trees that will obstruct our view." He leaned on a pole, waiting for her to respond.

At least he was deferring to her authority. Not that it mattered. She was wrong, and he was right, which didn't say much for her leadership abilities. She should've known which lift was better for viewing the course.

"Fine." Instead of side stepping to turn around, she pushed off in the wrong direction, pushed again to build momentum, then fishtailed to a stop, doing a one-eighty.

She skied back to Langston, who gave her an appreciative nod.

"You've always had mad skills on the slopes, Sans."

So had he. He also had mad skills between the sheets. Something she missed more and more each day she had to see him in the staff meetings.

Even more than missing the great sex, she missed *him*. So very, very much.

The sting of yearning that would never be satisfied bubbled up her throat, settling like acid against her tongue.

She swallowed it back down. "Let's—" Her voice cracked, and she cleared her throat. "Let's go." She pushed off, skied passed Cal and Jordyn, and caught the head of the cross-country trail that led to the other ski lift. She didn't stop, didn't look back until she arrived at the lift and stepped up to catch the next moving chair. Since it was a weekday morning, the chairs were mostly empty, as were the slopes.

Langston caught up to her just in time for the lift to scoop them off the ground.

The coldness of the chair bit into her butt and thighs, her thick leggings no match for the cold mountain altitude. "You're not going to wait for your little girlfriend?" Sandra blurted before she could stop herself.

Dammit. Even she could hear petty jealousy in her tone.

Langston stared out over the mountains, swinging his skis playfully. He chuckled. "You do still care."

She so did. "No. Just wondering why you're riding with me and not her. She adores you."

"Not interested." He looked behind them. "Besides, you were going so fast, I told them to hang back for safety reasons."

Sandra turned around, too. Jordyn and Cal were several chairs back. So far back that she couldn't make out their faces.

"Can't have members of my ski patrol getting hurt this close to the event." Langston's powerful thigh pressed into Sandra's as the lift took them high above the tree tops.

The air was so fresh and clean, as their frosty breaths fogged and swirled. The stark white mountains against the crystal blue sky was gorgeous. For the first time, the fact that she was going to be able to leave Red River for good struck a chord deep inside her. She'd felt trapped in the small mountain town for years, hoping and striving for the chance to start over somewhere else.

Now that it was within her grasp, it weighed heavily on her heart. Pressed in on her like darkness.

And the thought of never seeing Langston again made it hard to breathe. Nearly suffocated the life out of her.

With a gloved hand, she grasped the safety bar across her lap and forced the fresh mountain air into her lungs.

She wasn't even sure where she'd go when she left. Maybe a few hours south to Albuquerque. Maybe a few hours north to Denver. Wyoming, Utah, Montana. The possibilities were endless. All beautiful places, but none of them pulled at her heart, and she wasn't sure what her next step would be once she was free to leave Red River.

All she was sure of, at that moment, was that she was going to miss the beauty of *this* place. Not nearly as much as she'd miss the beautiful man sitting next to her, though.

"I wish we could stop the lifts just a little farther up. This is the best aerial view we have." He pointed to their right as the course came into view.

She pulled off a glove and retrieved a walkie-talkie from her jacket pocket. "I got this from the lodge as soon as the event was moved to Red River so I can communicate with them, the lift operators, base camp, or anyone else I need to speak to. Cell service is spotty, depending on where I'm at on the slopes, so this seemed to be a more efficient way of communicating. I'll make sure the rest of the staff is assigned one for the event. You and the ski patrol especially need them." When she pushed the button on the side of the device, it crackled to life. "This is Sandra. Stop the lift so we can inspect the barriers from above. Don't start it again until you hear from me."

It slowed, then came to a halt, the chair swaying gently with them suspended over the winter landscape.

Langston smiled.

Which made her heart skitter and skip.

"Good thinking. That's why you're the boss." He pointed to the course again.

She followed his outstretched hand. She leaned into him, her chin perched over his shoulder to get a better bead on what he was looking at.

Damn, he smelled good. The scent of masculine soap still clung to him. The tips of his hair curled around the bottom of his knit winter cap and glistened with the faintest hint of moisture. Obviously, he'd stepped out of the shower, pulled on clothes, and headed straight to the meeting.

"The course is farther away from this lift, but the main lift runs along the far side of the course." He leaned back against her and kept pointing. "Those are the trees that would've prevented us from seeing the spectator barriers from above. We have a better aerial view from this lift. We can inspect them closer when we're skiing down."

Her mouth was so close to the small strip of exposed skin just behind his ear that she had to bite her bottom lip to keep from kissing that spot. "I see what you mean." Her words came out as a whisper.

A visible shiver raced over him, and slowly, he angled his head to the side to look at her.

"I gotta say, Sans, I'm not getting an *I don't love you anymore* vibe. As much as I love that mouth of yours..." His chocolaty eyes turned lazy with lust and dropped to her lips. "It says one thing, but your body language says another." He turned, letting his lips hover just above hers. "Tell me I'm wrong."

She opened her mouth to speak, but the words wouldn't come

because he was so right. She'd lied to him about her feelings a few days ago. Why couldn't she do it now?

Before she could gather her wits, his warm lips captured hers. Soft yet firm. Patient yet demanding.

She melted into him, as she always did when he kissed her. His taste and the softness of his tongue against hers caused a storm to kick up low in her belly. Langston's touch turned her mind to mush and her body to putty.

Always had. Always would.

She sighed into his mouth, and he deepened the kiss.

How would she ever learn to live without him? Without *this?*

He snaked an arm around the back of the chair to encircle her shoulders. The other gloved hand slid up her thigh, settling in the center.

She moved her legs farther apart to give him more room.

His thick gloves only increased the friction. Even against the freezing cold chair, heat still ignited where he rubbed her until it scorched down her limbs.

She moaned.

"Yes, baby," he whispered against her lips, then took her mouth again in a wicked hot kiss.

Need cinched her core tighter and tighter as she reached for the glorious place that only Langston could take her.

She reached up to mold a gloved hand against his jaw...

And the walkie-talkie fell from her hand, plummeting to the earth below.

They both went deathly still.

Finally, she peered over their dangling legs and he did the same. The black walkie-talkie was a mere speck against the blanket of fresh powder.

"Oops," said Langston.

That had to be the understatement of the year.

They were stranded on a chairlift in the freezing cold, with no way to tell the lift operators to start them moving again. She was wearing leggings with no snow pants, and if someone didn't figure out fairly quickly that they needed help, she might end up with frostbite.

And it was all her fault.

Some boss she'd turned out to be. Not only had she put herself at risk, but she'd put three of her staff at risk as well.

Maybe the city council's skepticism over her capability and reliability had been spot on. If she couldn't go up a chairlift without endangering herself and three others, then she was probably the last person the council should've trusted to pull off an event as big as an international snowboarding championship.

And if they didn't get back to base camp without losing a few digits to frostbite...everyone was going to know it.

CHAPTER FIVE

"Do you have a cell phone with you?" Sandra asked Langston. "Mine is in my purse back at the lodge." They needed to call someone to get the lifts moving again ASAP.

Langston used his teeth to pull off a glove.

She grabbed it. "Let me hold that so it doesn't fall, too."

"Because you're so good at holding on to things these days?" His expression said he wasn't just talking about the walkie-talkie or the glove, but also the fact that she'd let go of him. He unzipped a cargo pocket on the side of his snow pants and withdrew his phone, tapping the screen.

She relaxed. "Thank God." She didn't want to add endangering herself and three others to her long list of transgressions against the people of Red River. Especially since this particular transgression would've actually been true.

Langston frowned at the phone.

Worry prickled over her skin, adding to the burn of the frozen chair against her backside. "What's wrong?"

"My phone is malfunctioning. Probably because of the single digit temperature." He stuffed the cell down the neck of his jacket and under his sweater. "My body heat will warm it up enough to start working. Give it a few minutes, and it'll be fine." His half-hearted smile didn't convince her in the least.

The prickle of worry turned to a stab of dread.

At least she could still feel something, so there was that.

She turned around and waved both arms, shouting to Cal and Jordyn to see if they had a phone. They were too far away to hear her, but in the distance, she could see the fuzziness of their arms waving back, as though it was all good.

Sandra turned back around and dropped her forehead against the safety bar.

"If they do have a phone, theirs won't likely be working either." Langston pressed a hand over the phone and held it firmly against his chest.

Holy hell, they were going to freeze to death all because of her. She should've taken the time to put on snow pants. She should've kept her wits about her and not let go of the walkie-talkie. Instead, she got distracted because Langston's mouth and hands made her ovaries—the shameless little hussies—want to ovulate right there on a chairlift!

The chair swayed gently as they gave the phone time to warm against his chest.

"I'm sorry." Sandra's voice cracked. "I screwed up."

"Nothing's screwed up." He reached into his sweater for the phone.

"I shouldn't have dropped the walkie-talkie." She blinked away the sting at the back of her eyes.

"I shouldn't have distracted you." He tapped on the screen. "Oh shit."

He let his hands fall to his lap and looked out over the mountainside, as though he was taking in the view. Or defeated.

Oh shit was right.

Gently, she tapped her forehead against the safety bar. The sound caused an idea to spring to life, and she bolted upright. "Okay, Mr. I Save Lives Like It's Just Another Day at The Office.

You know Morse Code, right?" Her teeth started to *tink, tink, tink* against each other.

He nodded, stuffing the phone back into his pants pocket. "I do."

"Good, because I can't feel my butt anymore." She handed him his glove. "See if your pole is long enough to reach the suspension cable."

He gave her a smart aleck grin—the kind that usually had her going hot all over and moist in places she couldn't talk about in public. "You already know how long my pole is."

Yes, yes, she did. All too well. And it was impressively long. "This isn't the time for jokes. I'm about to lose the backs of my legs and at least one ass cheek to frostbite. If your pole doesn't reach high enough, then one of our skis will so you can tap out an SOS."

He looked up to survey the suspension cable. "You're damn smart, you know that?" The approval in his voice wasn't lost on her.

Unfortunately, she didn't deserve it.

"A smart person wouldn't be stuck halfway up a mountain in subzero temperatures, wearing nothing but leggings." Now her teeth knocked against each other in a full-on chatter. "All because she couldn't resist the advances of a horny flight medic."

"True," he deadpanned.

At which point, she elbowed him in the ribs. Hard.

He broke into laughter. "Okay, okay." He lifted one ski pole high in the air and stretched up as far as he could. His long arms fit his tall frame, allowing the tip of the pole to reach the cable. He tapped out a message against the metal.

She had no idea if his tapping would vibrate far enough up or down the lift for someone to receive it, but it was worth a try.

When he was done, he unzipped his jacket and took off his sweater.

"Are you nuts?" She grabbed at his coat and tried to put it around his bare shoulders.

He shrugged her off. "Hell yes. I'm nuts for going along with your stupid idea to keep our relationship a secret all these years. Now, lift your ass."

"Um, what?" She scrunched her forehead. "And did you just call me stupid? Right after you called me damned smart?"

"I called your idea stupid because it is." He held up the sweater. "Let me do my job as safety officer and save that pretty little ass cheek of yours." His words came out shaky because his teeth were chattering, too.

She lifted one side of her butt. He slipped the sweater underneath, and she pulled it completely under her, tying it over the front of her thighs.

"Thank you." Her voice was a whisper, misty fog swirling with each breath.

"You're welcome." Langston pulled his coat on and zipped it up. "But don't thank me yet. No one has answered my SOS."

"Which is still my fault." She bit her ChapStick covered lip.

"It doesn't matter whose fault it is, Sans. People are people. We make mistakes. We get over them and move on. It's as simple as that." With a pole, he snapped off one ski, then the other. They fell to the earth below.

"What are you doing?" Sandra gasped.

"Saving both of our asses." Before she knew what was happening, he snapped off one of her skis and reached for the other. Just like his, they plummeted. He took both of his poles and anchored them between the slates of the back of the chair. "Gimme." He waggled a set of fingers at her poles until she gave them up, and he anchored them between the slates, too. Angling his body, he said, "Come here. I'll be the cocoon. Our combined body heat just might keep us from freezing to death."

"And I repeat, it's my fault we're in this mess." She snuggled against his chest and he wrapped his large frame around hers. The chair was only built for two, so they couldn't fully stretch out, but they curled into a twined human ball as best they could.

"And *I* repeat, it doesn't matter. I baited you into coming with me." He tightened his arms around her. "Hell, I was praying you'd come with me so I could spend time with you. I'm the one who couldn't keep my hands to myself on a fucking chairlift."

"True," she teased, parroting his words.

Dipping his head, he bit at her bottom lip.

She chuckled, because hell, it was either laugh or cry. When her giggles subsided, she said, "I wonder how Cal and Jordyn are." They were both just kids.

That's what Sandra had reduced herself to—she'd been jealous over a nineteen-year-old kid with a perky smile and springy curls.

Dear God, Sandra really was the loser Red River thought she was.

If she ever got off this lift, she'd follow through on her promise to put Red River in her rearview and leave Langston alone so he could finally find someone worthy. God knew she wasn't. The whole town knew it, too. Always had. He'd been the only one not willing to see it.

"Cal is training to be a firefighter, and he's been taught to survive situations far more dangerous than this." With one hand, he freed a pole. "Sit up for a sec." He tapped out another SOS, beating harder against the metal. Then returned the pole to its resting place and engulfed her again. "You can't keep carrying the blame on your shoulders for everything that goes wrong, Sans." His breaths were warm against her winter cap where he rested his chin. "People are always looking for someone to blame. It's human nature because it makes them feel better about their own problems. I'm not going to let you keep making yourself that scapegoat."

Her head popped up to look him in the eye. "What does that mean?"

The heavy breath he let out crystalized in the air around them. "It means—"

A loud pop caused both of them to jump, and an orange flame launched high in the air, arcing before it started to descend.

"Excellent." Langston didn't loosen his hold on her. "Cal must've heard the SOS and had a flare gun with him."

A flare gun was standard issue for ski patrol, but the trip up the lifts to inspect the course had been spontaneous, and she wasn't sure if Cal or Jordyn had thought to grab theirs.

"Hooray for gung-ho youngsters who want to save the world," Langston said. "He was far more prepared than I was. Maybe you should make him your safety officer."

Within seconds, the chair started to ascend toward the top of the mountain.

"Finish what you were going to say before the flare gun went off." She splayed a hand against Langston's chest. She wasn't moving until he explained himself.

His mocha eyes smoothed over her face, making the coldness abate. "I've done things your way for years, Sans. And what did that get me?"

He waited for her to answer.

She couldn't. She just couldn't.

She looked away, the hurt in his eyes stabbing at her heart. The wooden structure covering the drop off point, which everyone called the Shack, came into view.

Thank the baby Jesus.

"I'll tell you what it got me." Langston's voice turned a little harder. "It got me dumped anyway, and now I'm alone."

She let her eyes fall shut. "Langston, it's just the way it has to be."

He didn't hesitate. "Why?" He didn't wait for her to answer either. "Whether we're together or not, I'm not lying about how I feel about you anymore."

She opened her mouth to protest, but he covered it with a gloved finger.

"You broke up with me, so you don't have a say in what I do, or who I tell. I won't tell anyone about your dad, because it's not my story to tell. But I won't keep pretending you're not important to me. Not anymore." He gave her a nudge so they could sit up straight as the drop off got closer. "And that's just the way it has to be, Sans."

———

The first thing Sandra did when she got off the chairlift at the top of the mountain was wait for Cal and Jordyn. They were fine, and Jordyn looked at Cal with the same hero worship she'd had for Langston.

Sandra walked over to Langston, who had been talking to the lift operator. "Looks like you lost your fan club."

"Thank God." He went over and picked up the red phone hanging on the wall that connected directly to base camp.

Jordyn and Cal had had the sense to keep their skis on, so they could ski down the mountain on their own. As Jordyn pushed off toward the trail head at the top of a blue diamond run, Cal split off and skied back over to Sandra. "Sure you don't want us to go get baskets and pull you back to base camp?"

Sandra shook her head. She'd already put them in danger. She wasn't about to make them rescue her again. "You two go ahead. We'll get down another way."

"Who'd have thought a flare gun would get me the girl." He winked. "It worked like magic."

Sandra smiled. "Way to go, kiddo. See you two at the bottom."

Cal rejoined Jordyn, and they took off down the slopes together.

Langston hung up the phone and came over. "I called someone to come get us on snowmobiles. I didn't think you'd want to ride back down on the lift without snow pants."

"Good call," she said. "I've had enough of that for one day." She wrapped both arms around herself.

"You okay?" He rubbed her arms.

She lifted a shoulder. "I've been through worse." She didn't need to explain. Langston was the only person in Red River who knew the whole truth about what she'd been through. "I was pretty stupid for hitting the slopes without proper gear." She shook one foot, then the other. "I'm starting to feel my toes again, though. Maybe the rest of the feeling in my legs will come back if I go take a hot bath."

"I can help with that." His smoky eyes said he wanted her.

"Langston," she whispered. "Don't tell anyone about us. It'll only make things worse."

The sound of snowmobiles buzzed in the distance.

"Worse for who, Sans? Maybe you're just embarrassed for anyone to know you're with me."

"Of course, I'm not embarrassed," she huffed. Wanting to keep their affair between just the two of them was never about her embarrassment. It had always been about his.

"After all these years, I've gotta wonder."

Two snowmobiles appeared over a rise on a flat beginner's run and made their way over to Sandra and Langston.

He rolled a finger in a mock bow. "Your chariot awaits."

By the time they were safely at the bottom of the mountain, it was obvious the flare gun had alerted more than just the lift operators. A crowd of locals had already gathered.

Seriously?

Sandra gathered her courage for the onslaught.

Sure enough, they were greeted with a flood of questions the second she and Langston hopped off the snowmobiles.

This town, always with the questions. Always a crowd ready to pounce on Sandra's every mistake. This time she was guilty as hell.

"What happened?" someone asked from the back of the crowd.

Sandra put on a brave face. "It was my—"

"I got distracted," Langston interrupted. "It was all my doing."

"How'd you survive the cold in those pants?" someone else shouted.

Langston unzipped his coat, revealing his bare chest.

His broad, bare, badass chest.

The crowd went quiet.

He reached down and untied his sweater from around Sandra's

legs. "We shared body heat." He shucked his coat long enough to pull the sweater over his head, then he put on the coat again. He draped an arm around her shoulders.

"Langston, *please*," she whispered.

"You can say please again once we get to my place." He tightened his grip, pulling her closer, and leaned down so only she could hear. "Hopefully, you'll be begging me to take you while we're in a hot bath."

She swallowed. He was really going to do this. After so many years of her trying to protect him.

"We can answer questions later." He held up a hand. "Right now, I'm taking my girl home so she can warm up."

Murmurs rippled through the crowd.

His girl.

Pride swelled in her chest.

She'd always wondered how it would feel to hear those words in public.

Without another word, Langston led her away, but stopped next to Cal and lifted his hand in the air like a champion. "This is the man of the hour. We could've gotten severe frostbite or worse if he hadn't thought to bring his flare gun."

Langston headed to the parking lot with Sandra tucked under his arm. They stopped only once to glance over a shoulder at Cal. The crowd had surrounded him, abuzz with excitement over his new hero status.

Langston and Sandra chuckled, got in his truck, and went to go take that steaming hot bath.

CHAPTER SIX

"We still have to inspect the barriers," Sandra said, pulling off her clothes in Langston's master bathroom.

He sat on the side of the tub and tested the running water, wearing nothing but jeans. "We've got all day. First, I want you to warm up..." He shot her a wicked sexy smile with a naughty gleam in his eyes. "Both in the tub of hot water and in bed, then we're going to get a late lunch at Joe's. Together."

Fear lanced through her, making her stomach do a flip-flop. They'd never gone out together in public unless she'd made it look like it was a no-strings-attached hook-up.

"After that, I'll take you home to get your ski gear and we can go check the barriers." He went to the cabinet under one of the sinks and pulled out a bottle of bubble bath. "I got this for you." He poured a stream of the purple liquid under the running water and it instantly foamed into a thick layer.

The scent of lavender filled the room and settled over her. She breathed it in, some of the tension in her shoulders releasing.

She loved hot bubble baths. "Lavender's my favorite." She unhooked her bra and let the lace hover over her breasts. No one had ever accused her of being flat chested, that was for sure. She'd been blessed in that department, if she did say so herself.

"I know." Hunger flared in his eyes. "That's why I bought it, but you broke up with me before we could make good use of it."

"I'm sorry," she whispered. "Maybe I can make it up to you." With a swish of one shoulder then the other, the thin straps slid down her arms, and the bra fell to the floor.

His gaze turned smoky. With his arms folded over his chest and his bare feet crossed at the ankles, he let his eyes lick over her all the way to her painted, curling toes, leaving a trail of burning heat against her skin. When they started the journey upward again, they snagged on the lace triangle just above her thighs.

He rolled an index finger in a *keep it going* gesture. "I'm enjoying this. Especially since it's the first time you haven't made it a point to sneak in and out of my house without being seen."

Another pang of fear tightened her chest. "That's what I'm afraid of. You've never been on the wrong end of Red River gossip. That might change now that people know about us."

Keeping their relationship a secret was one thing, but letting the world know they were lovers who'd been committed to each other for a long time might be entirely different. She was used to being scorned. He wasn't, and it was going to cut deep to watch it happen to him.

She'd created an impossible situation. On top of the pain he might experience from people in town because of her, she was going to inflict even more when she told him she'd planned to close her shop so she could make a quick exit from Red River after the snowboarding championship was over and done.

But with him sitting there, looking at her with so much lust... so much love, she didn't have the heart to spoil the moment. "What will your sister say? Your friends? Your *parents?*"

"I don't care." Langston pushed off the tub. "I'm a grown ass man who doesn't need permission to love someone."

Sandra's pulse kicked. They'd loved each other a long time, words that had come easily in secret. How would those beautiful words affect them now that their relationship was out in the open?

"Maybe we should take this slow," she said.

He stopped within reach but didn't touch her. Instead, he tilted his head forward so his warm breaths caressed over her cheeks. "Slow? We've been together for years. You don't think that's slow enough?"

She shrugged. "I mean, now that people know about us, maybe we should reveal our feelings a little at a time. This will be new to everyone in town. I'm not sure I want to expose more than we have to." She tried to ignore the flash of heat that ignited at her core as he hooked his thumbs into the elastic waist of her lace panties. "At least not all at once." How were people going to react when they knew she and Langston had been hiding the truth for years?

"I'm done lying about us." He nipped at the corner of her mouth, his voice turning husky. "As for revealing and exposing..." With a push of his fingers, her panties pooled at her feet. "The more we reveal and expose, the better, as far as I'm concerned."

He still didn't take that final step to close the space between them. One palm closed over her full breast, kneading and massaging until her flesh ached under his touch. Her head fell back, and her eyes closed.

"I missed seeing you like this." His voice was a hungry whisper as he pinched a hardened nipple between a thumb and forefinger.

A hiss of pleasure slipped through her parted lips.

"I missed hearing you like this." His head dipped to take the other nipple between his teeth. He toyed with it, then nipped with just enough pressure to make her squirm.

"*Langston, please.*" Her voice was desperate and distant, as though she wasn't the one speaking.

"I told you on the slopes you'd beg." His warm breaths against her throbbing flesh made a shiver skate over her.

She fisted his hair at the back of his head and pulled his mouth back to her aching breast. "You got what you wanted. I'm begging."

He swiped his tongue over her rock-hard peak, then chuckled, grabbing her hand to pull her toward the tub. "What I want isn't the point. Not even close."

No, it never had been with Langston. That was the reason he'd gone along with her insistence to keep their relationship under the radar.

Once they were standing next to the steaming bath, he flicked open the button of his jeans and kicked them off.

She couldn't help it. She couldn't. Her gaze slid over every delicious inch of him. Good Lord but the man was gorgeous. Muscled thighs. Tight abs. Broad shoulders. The kind of man that should be Mr. February on a sexy first responders' calendar.

Ah hell. Langston's body was so perfect, he could have an entire calendar all to himself, gracing the pages of every month.

Admiration must've reflected in her eyes, because a satisfied smile turned up one corner of his mouth. "I want to give you what you want. What you deserve. Why else would I buy bubble bath?"

"For yourself?" she teased. "You seem like a bubble bath kind of guy." He so didn't.

"Don't push your luck. I'm willing to take one with you and only you. Just do *not* tell anyone about this, especially my friends and family." He held out a hand. "Dudes don't do bubble baths and live to tell the tale. Plus, it would give my sister a lifetime of ammunition to use against me at family gatherings."

Family gatherings. *Brooks* family gatherings.

Her heart did a *thumpity thump thump*.

"Stop it," he scolded, his hand still outstretched. "You're thinking too much. I can see it all over your face." He waggled his fingers.

Sandra placed her hand in his and stepped into the tub.

He slid in behind her and encased her with those powerful, muscled thighs.

She leaned back against his chest and let the water's heat soak into her skin. Langston's legs, arms, and stomach weren't the only things that were muscled and hard as granite. His impressive shaft was firm against her lower back.

"What I want right now is for you to be wrapped around me, so I feel safe." She reached back and slid both hands up his neck until they disappeared in his hair. She turned her head and pulled his mouth to hers. "And inside me so I feel good."

The low growl in his chest rumbled against her back.

"I can do both while we're soaking in this tub." One arm slipped around to her front and cupped her breast.

"That's a nice trick." Her fingers slid through his silky curls. "You always were a magician with those hands."

He took the cuff of her ear between his teeth and nibbled. "Don't forget my tongue." He took her chin between a thumb and finger and turned her face up to his. His mouth crushed down on hers, and he eased his other hand down her thigh, covering the triangle of curls between her legs. His large frame made his arms more than long enough to reach the promised land, and he eased a finger inside of her.

She arched back against him and moaned.

"*Fuck's sake, woman,*" he groaned. "You're slick." His thumb circled her clit, causing another moan to tumble through her lips.

"You're hard," she ground out, her eyes closed against the sensation of his fingers filling her and caressing her throbbing nub at the same time. "And I want you."

"Let me work my magic in the tub first." He feathered hot yet sweet kisses behind her ear, his warm breaths causing her skin to pebble, even in the hot water.

His fingers worked her flesh, delving, circling, curling into the deepest, most intimate part of her.

The first whisper of orgasm started at her core, building like a storm with each thrust of his fingers. Gaining strength with each circle of his thumb.

"Jesus, you're so fucking beautiful like this." His words were an urgent whisper, the desire in his voice almost painful. "I want to taste you here." He increased the pressure of his thumb against her clit, plunged two fingers inside of her to their hilt, and they did a little twist and curl number.

A powerful orgasm barreled through her, and she shattered into a million little pieces. *"Oh, God,"* she breathed out as she soared above the clouds. Her insides convulsed around his fingers as she fought to draw air into her locked lungs. "How..." she panted out. "How do you do that to me?"

When the last trembles of bliss subsided, he wrapped her up in his arms. "It's just the way it's always been between us, don't you think? So good that there is no rational explanation."

She nodded, her breathing still rushed and irregular. Her pulse still racing like mad.

"After all these years, it's how I know we're meant to be. If we weren't, the magic, as you put it, would've worn off already." He placed a kiss in her hair.

A whine came from the door.

"Hey there, Zeus," she greeted the gigantic dog, and he trotted to the tub.

"I think he's glad to see me." She scratched behind his ear, and he licked warm water off her forearm.

"Mine, Zeus." Langston brought her wrist to his lips and feathered kisses along the inside.

Desire sprang to life again and shimmied through her.

"Zeus," Langston said between kisses. "Laundry room. Now, boy."

Zeus whined and trotted out of the bathroom.

"Good boy." Sandra turned in Langston's arms, giving him a naughty smile. "And I'm not talking about the dog." She trailed hot, open-mouthed kisses down his neck, over his collarbone, and across his hard pecs to the water's edge. She straddled him, his hard length pulsing at her entrance. "You deserve a treat."

His greedy stare cut through the water's misty steam, and he molded both palms over her breasts. "You already owe me for breaking up with me." Raising up, his hot mouth closed around a nipple and he suckled it into a hard mound.

She cried out.

"Now I've earned a treat, too?" He chuckled against her nipple, then circled the tip with his tongue. "Your list of debts is growing." He moved to the other breast and did the same.

She was lost in the pleasure. "Then we better get started." With one fluid movement, she sank onto him, encasing his silky steel like a sheath.

He bit off a curse word, his jaw twitching.

She braced her palms against his chest, slowly, lifted until she was at his tip, circled her hips, then plunged down on him again.

That time he couldn't hold back the words. "That's so damn good, babe."

He filled her so completely, so perfectly, that her breathing grew ragged as she did the same thing once, twice. Over and over, finding a rhythm that made every nerve ending hum with electricity.

His fingers dug into the cheeks of her ass, the sting so sweet that it made her want to weep, as he guided her up and down his length.

As she made love to him and clutched at his shoulders, his muscled chest moved under her touch. Shifting and tensing, his skin hot and sleek with moisture. Droplets of water starred his beautiful lashes.

"*Oh*," she whimpered. "I'm close, Langston."

"That's it, babe." One set of fingers dug deeper into her butt and the other found her clit and rubbed. He increased the speed of their rhythm, water sloshing over the sides of the tub.

He was so big, so skilled that it didn't take long for another explosive orgasm to overtake her. He took her mouth with his in a white-hot kiss as he found his release, too, his flesh pulsing inside of her until she thought she'd scream.

She wrapped her arms around his head and buried her face in his hair.

They stayed like that for a long time. Sandra wasn't sure how long. Minutes? Hours? All she knew was that she wanted to spend a lifetime with him, just like this, in his arms.

In his forever.

Finally, Langston had to be the one to break the spell. "The water's getting cold." His fingers caressed up and down her spine, making it tingle.

She leaned back and brushed a damp curl off his forehead. "How about we get in bed, and I'll pay off another debt on my list?"

With quick, powerful movements that had water splashing out of the tub, Langston stood up and hauled her with him, sweeping her up into his arms. He stepped out of the tub. "Best idea I've heard in a long time."

Without drying off, they went to bed, and she gave him that treat. Then he rode her fast and hard until they both were satiated and complete.

Afterwards, he flipped onto his back and pulled her against his chest. The steady rhythm of his heartbeat against her cheek was the most wonderful thing she'd ever felt. Sure, they'd slept in that position many, many times. But today. Today was the start of something special. The beginning of something much better than they'd had in the past.

She didn't have to hide her feelings for him anymore. Didn't have to pretend to be interested in other men, just to distract others from the truth.

He stroked her hair. "I knew you really didn't mean it when you said you didn't love me, didn't want me."

Her mouth turned to cotton, and her throat closed against the pain she'd caused him. Caused both of them. She nodded against his chest, unable to speak.

He folded an arm under his head, and kept stroking her hair from the top all the way to the ends of her long wavy locks.

Each stroke lulled her deeper and deeper into a dreamy state of bliss. She traced the lines of his firm stomach with the tip of an index finger.

He placed a soft, loving kiss on the top of her head. "After all the years I've waited, I knew you wouldn't stab me in the heart." He snorted. "I'm embarrassed to admit it, but when you broke up with me, I had visions of you skipping town. Leaving me flat, like your father did you."

Her lungs stopped working, and her hand stilled against his chest.

"But I knew you didn't have it in you to be so cruel. That's not who you are." His arms circled her, and he held her close. "I guess I was just scared. My life has worked out pretty well so far, except for not being able to have a normal relationship with you. Deep down, I didn't want to believe that this..." He waggled a finger back and forth between them, then went back to holding her. "This was what I wanted most in life, but it might be the one thing that wouldn't work out for me. I was scared to face the heartbreak. I'm a dude. We're not good with that sort of thing. I'm so sorry I doubted you, Sans."

Oh. Dear Lord. What had she done? Skipping town was exactly what she'd planned. Sure, for the right reasons, unlike her father. Her plan was to *help* Langston by leaving Red River, not to throw him under the bus.

For the first time, she let herself fully see the situation through his eyes.

It wasn't pretty. What he'd just revealed, told her that her plan to leave town...leave him, was going to hurt him even more than she'd thought. It had been unfair. Unwise.

Unforgiveable.

She squeezed her eyes shut to block out the truth.

Unfortunately, she'd proven herself right. He deserved better than her. He just didn't see it yet. He would, though, as soon as she found the right time to tell him everything.

CHAPTER SEVEN

Later that afternoon, they stepped into Cotton Eyed Joe's. Since it was between the lunch rush and dinner hour, the place wasn't crowded, but the tables and booths that were filled with customers stilled. Stared.

And Sandra stiffened into a plank of wood at his side.

Langston knew right away the customers were mostly locals. Wasn't hard to spot the tourists. In the winter, they were either on the slopes or walking along Main Street in full-on ski or snowboarding gear. Plus, in a town the size of Red River, everybody knew one another.

He placed a hand at the small of Sandra's back and followed the hostess. Besides the peanut shells crunching under their all-weather boots, the place was silent. Which was why the whispers that started as they crossed the room were so much more noticeable than he'd ever remembered.

Sandra tensed under the palm of his hand, but kept her chin lifted. Only the slight quiver of her bottom lip gave away the anxiety that must've been racing through her.

For the first time, he realized just how awful it must've been for Sandra for so many years. The pressure. The shame. Sure, he'd always known she'd had a rough road to travel after her father let her take the blame for his addiction and all the bad things he'd done to support his drug problem. But this? This was different than he'd imagined. The stares and whispers had him wanting to pull at his collar and go hide in a corner.

Which was the reason he had to put a stop to it once and for all.

The coldness of guilt and regret slid through his veins, turning him to ice.

No more.

It ended today, and anyone who had a problem with Sandra could speak to him personally. Anyone who wanted to hurt her with words or actions could answer to him personally, too.

He increased the pressure at the small of her back to offer some comfort as they followed the hostess.

Sandra shot a nervous glance at him, and he nodded to communicate his support. She wasn't going to be alone in life ever again. He would always be there for her, no matter what.

The hostess led them past the tables and booths that lined the wall, heading toward the back of the large room.

Depending on the day and hour, the town's famed watering hole was more of a restaurant slash saloon slash dance hall, where everybody gathered to eat, drink, and catch up on gossip. Gossip was common in small towns. Hell, it was common among humans regardless of the community's population, but in a close-knit place like Red River, gossip was practically an art.

Langston needed to make sure Sandra was no longer the topic of negative conversation.

The hostess led them to a booth against the far wall, putting distance between them and most of the other patrons.

"Actually..." He pulled his phone from his pocket and pretended to read a text. "Others are joining us. Can we sit over there?" He pointed to a table for eight in the center of the room, where everyone could see them. Where they'd be the center of attention.

Sandra's eyes rounded.

He gave her a reassuring wink. "Let me get a headcount." He

fired off an emergency text to all of his friends with very little explanation. Not much was needed. His friends would be there for him, with no questions asked, so his message simply said *SOS, meet me and my girl Sandra Edwards at Joe's. Need to stop the wagging tongues.* They'd probably be just as surprised as the rest of Red River, but they wouldn't show it. He was sure of that much. "That table should work for us, but if we need more seats, we can push two tables together." He stuffed the phone into his pocket and grinned at the hostess, sending a clear message that his request was non-negotiable.

The hostess seated them and left menus around the table.

"Who's coming?" Sandra whispered.

Langston leaned over so his lips were a breath from hers. "I don't know exactly, but there's power in numbers. When people in my inner circle show their support, it will scare off the gossipers." He placed a soft kiss on her lips. Mainly to show the world that she was his, but also because he was so damn relieved they weren't hiding anymore.

When he broke the kiss and looked over her shoulder, more heads had turned, and more murmurs were rounding the room.

"I don't know who you texted or what you said to them, but are you sure they'll show if you're with me?" Her eyes darted around the room, and she fidgeted with her napkin.

He let out a sigh that was laced with sadness. Sadness for all she'd obviously suffered without him fully realizing how bad it must've been for her. "I'm certain of it." Gently, he grasped a lock of her beautiful hair and fingered it. It was so soft against his callused fingertips. Just like her. Yet she'd always had to be so tough, so thick skinned just to survive. "You're one of us now. You should've been from the beginning, but I let the charade continue far too long. Now that we're out in the open as a couple, my friends won't let you down. They'll put their support behind us."

Her mouth curved into a reluctant smile that said she wasn't entirely convinced. "I've given most of them a reason to dislike me at some point or another."

Langston nodded. "I know." She'd flirted with all of his friends before they married, just for show. To throw people off so her relationship with Langston could stay off the grid. If they only knew, he was the only person she'd ever been with. "Doesn't matter. We're together, and the past is in the past." He knew his friends would agree because each one of them had faced their own demons and had come out on the other side stronger. Happier.

Most importantly, they'd each found love in the process, so he was certain they'd offer their acceptance of Sandra without reservation because he'd done the same for them.

The front door swung open, and in walked Doc Holloway and his wife, Angelique—Red River's brilliant legal mind who attracted business from all over the state. Angelique gave Sandra a peck on the cheek, as though they were long lost friends, before they took seats across the table.

At the friendly greeting, Sandra seemed to relax a little.

"I don't know if you texted Coop and Ella, but they're out of town," Angelique said, placing a napkin in her lap.

Langston nodded. He'd been able to slide into the safety officer's position, spend more time with Sandra, and chip away at her stubbornness because of Cooper Wells' accident.

Doc Holloway spoke up. While his nickname made him sound like a little old man, Blake Holloway was about the same age as the rest of the group. "There isn't an orthopedic surgeon in this area who can handle a break as bad as Coop's. It's going to be a long road to recovery."

"I'm sorry to hear that," Sandra said, her voice wavering.

"Thanks for coming," Langston said. The Holloways and the Wells hadn't grown up in Red River, but they were trusted friends all the same.

"Sure thing." Angelique winked.

"Any time," Doc Holloway said. "I'm going to get my order to go, though." He glanced at his watch. "I've got a patient in twenty minutes."

With another swing of the door, Talmadge Oaks—hometown

kid who grew up to become a leader in green architecture—and his wife, Miranda, walked in and marched straight over to Sandra to give her a hug.

"I'm starved," said Miranda as she claimed a seat, her volume turned up unusually high. High enough for most of the other customers to hear. "I missed lunch because the phone at the inn hasn't stopped ringing, thanks to Sandra. The snowboarding championship is bringing so much extra tourism to town this season, it's going to be the best year I've had since I bought the Bea in the Bonnet Inn." Miranda perused the menu.

Langston knew the second Sandra figured out that his text message to his friends hadn't just been a casual invitation to lunch. It was meant to send a message to the entire town.

Her head slowly turned, and her eyes hooked into his. Those beautiful big eyes glistened with moisture under the overhead lights.

With an arm still draped around the back of her chair, he smiled back and caressed her shoulder with his fingertips. "It's what we do," he whispered with a shrug. It was called friendship. And another pang of regret pierced his chest, as though someone was stabbing him in the heart with an icepick. Sandra didn't have real friends, except him, because she'd kept everyone else at a distance.

The last couple to walk through the front door was his sister, Lorenda, and her husband, Mitchell. Lorenda hugged Sandra and tousled Langston's hair like he was a kid, then she and Mitchell occupied the last two vacant chairs.

Miranda didn't look up from her menu. "The key is to not let them win," she said low enough so only their table could hear. "Show them who's boss, and they'll respect you for it."

And that was why he loved this group of people. They didn't know the details, and they didn't care to know. All they cared about was helping each other the way true friends should.

The old saying that when a person gets to the end of their days, they're lucky if they have a handful of tried and true friends who've stuck with them through the shitstorm called life...

Well, this was Langston's handful of friends, and now they were obviously Sandra's, too.

"I..." Sandra looked around, as though she was making sure no one was listening. In a low voice, she said, "I've been trying to earn my way back into their good graces for years by working hard. Hasn't worked so far."

Langston was determined to change that, especially now that they could actually have a real relationship out in the open. A real future together as a couple.

Angelique studied her menu, too. "Without breaking client-attorney privilege, want to know what I've learned by practicing law in a small town?" She didn't wait for an answer. "Everybody has a secret. Small towns are like soap operas."

Mitchell nodded. "True. You wouldn't believe some of the stuff I've seen since I became deputy sheriff."

Lorenda spoke up. "You can't make up some of the stuff that's gone down in this town." She cuddled into Mitchell's side. "I should know. I married the town bad boy, but it worked out well for me. And ask me if I care what anyone else thinks."

The server interrupted them long enough to take their orders.

When they were alone again, Langston said, "I think what they're trying to say is, take charge of your life. Stop giving others power over you." His fingers tightened around her shoulder. He wanted Sandra to finally stop living in the shadows, but more importantly, he wanted *her* to want that for herself. For *them* as a couple. He'd been trying to tell her as much for a long time. Now that he'd outed them, maybe she'd finally listen. "People are the same, no matter where you go or where you live."

Tension rippled through her, and she let out a small gasp.

He let his gaze settle on her, but she wouldn't look at him.

He caressed the back of her neck with a thumb. "If you let them, they'll make you a victim. If you take that power away, they'll treat you the way you've deserved to be treated all along."

The server appeared with a tray. She delivered Doc Holloway's food in a to-go box, then passed out the rest of their meals.

Lorenda tapped a fork against her glass of tea. "Before Doc leaves, I want to propose a toast." Not only did she speak loud enough for everyone at Joe's to hear, but the restaurant down the street could've probably heard his sister, too, which had Langston smiling. "The entire town owes Sandra Edwards a huge thank you for bringing this snowboarding championship to Red River. It's pouring even more money into our local economy, gaining Red River international recognition and exposure, and putting us on the map as one of the most beautiful resort towns in the Rockies." Lorenda lifted her glass. "Heck, I've sold more real estate this winter than the last five winters combined, and Brooks Real Estate owes it all to you, Sandra."

Miranda lifted her glass. "I love Red River, but I especially love that we've got people like Sandra working hard to make our town a better place." Her voice was just as loud as Lorenda's had been.

The whole table toasted, each with something nice to say about his girl.

Hell, in a matter of minutes, they'd become Sandra's own private cheer squad, and the rest of the customers had seemed to lose interest and had gone back to their own conversations.

His stare settled on Sandra again, and his chest tightened.

They'd been together long enough for him to know when something was bothering her. He bent and whispered in her ear, "Crisis averted. Look around. No one in the restaurant seems to care that we're together. And my friends and sister wouldn't be doing this if they disapproved of us seeing each other."

Sandra blinked, staring up at him, and wetness shimmered in her eyes.

He wrinkled his brow.

They were free. No more hiding. No more secrets. No more misleading others.

So why did the expression on her face say that she was more worried than ever?

CHAPTER EIGHT

Two days before the championship began, Sandra got to the shop extra early to put out new inventory from her storeroom and continue training the new temporary employees who would be manning the store during the event.

Every night since they'd been stranded on the chairlift, she'd left the shop and spent those hours in bed with Langston, without having to sneak into his place or smuggle him into hers. It was magical and surreal, and she didn't want it to end. So she'd kept telling herself that it would be best to wait until after the championship was over to confess that she'd been planning to leave Red River without telling him. She was too preoccupied with running a business and organizing the snowboarding championship. He was too busy being magnificent.

Truth was she hadn't had the heart to hurt him all over again now that their relationship was finally out in the open.

Hell.

She dropped her face into her hands. *That* wasn't even the whole truth. The whole truth was she'd been too chickenshit to tell him, because of the betrayal she knew she'd see in his beautiful chocolaty eyes, and because of the shame she felt.

With a box cutter, she opened one of the few containers of new winter gear left in her storeroom.

Her goal to reduce her inventory before shutting the shop's doors had worked beautifully. Tourists and competitors had poured into town during the past week, and every store and restaurant along Main Street was busy from the moment they opened until they finally flipped off their lights and went home at the end of the work day.

She tossed a handful of hangers into the box and hauled it to the retail area. She stuffed a hanger inside the neck of a ski jacket and jammed it onto a rack. Then the next, and the next.

"I'm such a loser," she mumbled out loud as she worked her way through the box of new gear. Then she went and got another box.

She'd finally gotten the things in life she never thought she'd be lucky enough to have—acceptance from a close group of friends who supported each other, and a real chance to have a life with the man she'd loved since she was a teenager—and she'd screwed it up already.

As the sun rose higher and spilled through the shop windows, the doorbell jingled. One of her new employees walked in to work the morning shift.

"Morning, Avery," Sandra said.

Avery was already on her phone. "Morning, Ms. Edwards."

Sandra rubbed the corners of her eyes with a thumb and forefinger. "I told you to call me Sandra." *Ms. Edwards* made her feel like a little old lady who should be using a walker. It also highlighted the fact that she was still single and might always be, unless Langston could eventually forgive her.

Of course, to earn his forgiveness, she'd actually have to take responsibility and tell him everything. And that group of supportive friends? They might not be so supportive once they found out she'd planned to leave their buddy without so much as a parting goodbye. Sandra doubted any amount of explaining that she'd had his best interest at heart would help.

"Finish restocking the racks for me. I need to make a few calls, then I'll watch you open the register." She'd just shown Avery the opening procedures yesterday, and it might take a few tries to remember all of the steps.

Avery swung a denim purse off one shoulder and stored it behind the register, then Sandra handed off the hangers to her.

Sandra went to the register and got her phone from behind the counter. She'd been trying to reach her landlord all week. She'd left messages. Sent emails. Gone to the landlord's office personally. But hadn't gotten a response except an auto generated email that said *Sorry, I'm out of the office until...*

Today. Mrs. Tillerson would be back in town today, and hopefully open for business at the ass crack of dawn since she'd been on vacation for what seemed like an eternity.

Sandra tapped in Mrs. Tillerson's phone number and listened to it ring. Once, twice—

It went to voicemail again.

Sandra blew out a frustrated sigh and leaned a hip against the counter to wait for the tone. "Um, hello, Mrs. Tillerson. It's Sandra Edwards again. I really, *really* need to talk to you about letting this retail space go. I've changed my mind and would like to discuss renewing my lease."

What if it was too late? What if the space had already been leased to someone else?

Sandra discarded her phone onto the counter. She was being ridiculous.

If Mrs. Tillerson had been on vacation and couldn't return Sandra's messages, then she hadn't been around to lease the space to anyone else either. It was going to be fine. It would all work out, and she'd renew her lease, order new inventory, and she and Langston would live a long and happy life together. Because he loved her and knew that she loved him, and love conquered all.

And unicorns were real.

Now she wasn't just being ridiculous, she was being down right stupid.

"All done with restocking, but we're running low on ski gloves and there's none in the storeroom." Avery joined her at the register.

Sandra nodded. "I'll order more this week." Just as soon as she spoke to the landlord and knew for sure she'd still have a shop to sell them in. "I'm a little behind because of the championship, and we've sold more than I expected."

"Probably because you've been running such great sales," Avery said.

Right. "Speaking of, when I'm gone to the daily staff meeting over at the lodge, take down the sale signs. All the new merchandise goes back to full price today."

Sandra watched Avery open the register and go through the rest of the opening procedures. As soon as the shop opened for business, customers filled the store.

Twenty minutes before she had to leave for the morning event staff meeting, she finished fitting a pair of snowboarders with new top-of-the-line goggles. As she rang up their purchases, the front doorbell jingled.

Langston stepped inside, looking like his usual rugged, hot self and holding a white bag from the Ostergaard's and a coffee carrier with two cups in it.

Her insides sighed, and she felt it down to her toes.

"I thought we could have coffee, then I'll give you a ride to the meeting." He gave her that smartass, sexy as hell smile that she loved so much, and held up the coffee and paper bag.

"God, I love you," she said to Langston as she handed the customers their merchandise.

As soon as the shoppers left the store, he said, "You just want me because I give you scones." He sat the treats down on the counter. "Among other things." He waggled his brows at her.

She shrugged playfully. "Mostly the scones."

He laid a smokin' hot kiss on her, then breathed against her lips, "I love you, too."

Saying it out loud with customers in her store and an employee within earshot was even more incredible than she'd dreamt. But she had to bust his chops anyway, because he liked it when she challenged him. "When I said 'I love you,' I was talking to the bag of scones."

He reached around and pinched her ass.

The tinkle of the bell didn't faze either of them. They stayed toe-to-toe, their noses touching and their eyes locking.

"Good morning, Sandra."

A familiar, frazzled voice had Sandra's head snapping back like she'd been slapped.

"Mrs. Tillerson!" Sandra stumbled back and had to grab onto the counter to keep her balance.

"Hello, Langston," the landlord said. "As soon as I got back into town yesterday evening, I heard about you two. Congratulations! You're the talk of the town."

Of course, they were.

She looked at them thoughtfully. "You know, I never would've thought of getting you two together, but you make the perfect couple."

Oh, what those words of acceptance meant, coming from a respected member of Red River's business community. Except Sandra couldn't enjoy the victory. Not now, when her whole world might crumble.

"I wasn't expecting you." Sandra sidestepped around Langston and hurried to Mrs. Tillerson, trying to hustle her to the door. "How about I stop by your office in a few hours."

Creases appeared between Langston's eyes as he watched her.

Mrs. Tillerson didn't budge. "Oh, no, hon." She waved a hand in the air. "Your messages sounded more and more frantic as I listened to each of them late last night." She reached into her satchel. "All twenty-four of them."

"No." Sandra fought to control the desperation in her voice. "I mean, no, I should come by later." She pushed the front door open. "The shop is busy right now, and we're about to leave for a staff meeting. I'll stop in as soon as I'm done. Promise."

"Sure, sure." Mrs. Tillerson withdrew a manila envelope from her satchel. "I'll just drop off the new lease now, and you can bring the signed copy by whenever it's convenient. I'm just glad you changed your mind about staying in town. We need savvy businesswomen like you in Red River." She held out the envelope.

Sandra's eyes slid shut.

When she opened them, it wasn't Mrs. Tillerson's encouraging smile that had Sandra's blood kicking wildly through her veins. No, that would've made her life too easy. It would've made the moment too good.

It was the hurt in Langston's eyes and the betrayal in his expression that had her heart doing double time. Slowly, she reached for the envelope as though it might burn when she touched it.

"Well, see you later." Mrs. Tillerson gave both of them a friendly smile. "And good luck to you with everything. The championship..." Obviously, confused by the sudden tension that filled the air around them, her gaze shifted between Sandra and Langston. "And with each other."

When she pushed the door open and left, the cold gust of air that blew in was nothing compared to the ice pumping through Sandra's veins.

It took her several long moments to tear her stare from the envelope in her hands.

"Langston." She took a step toward him, trying to explain.

He lifted a hand. "Don't. Just don't." He stepped around the counter and walked in her direction.

Her heart filled with hope.

But he didn't come to her. Instead, he stepped up to the door and put his hand against it, obviously to leave.

And Sandra knew he wasn't just leaving the shop. He was likely leaving *her*.

"You *were* going to desert me. After all the years I..." He blew out a breath and shook his head. "All this time, you've been telling me that you were my dirty little secret. It hasn't really mattered to you that I've never considered you anything less than the love of my life." He stared at the floor for a beat.

She reached out to touch his arm. "Langston—"

He took a step back, and her heart jumped to her throat. "I was waiting for the right time to tell you. I'm sor—"

"Do not tell me you're sorry," he said through gritted teeth, the pain and anger in his voice nearly knocking her to her knees. "Not after it turns out that I've been *your* dirty little secret. I was just too stupid to see it."

Sandra watched him push through the door and vanish, along with her happiness and her future.

CHAPTER NINE

Sandra got her game face on.

She stood in front of the soaring two-story glass window of the lodge. A crowd formed on the bunny slope, where the opening ceremony was set up and ready to begin in less than an hour.

It was early March now, and today was the day. She lifted her chin and squared her shoulders.

She'd done it. She'd pulled off an international event with very little time to plan and limited resources beyond her wits and work ethic. More importantly, she'd done an extraordinary job that just might keep the ISA coming back every year, and might even catch the eye of other professional winter sports organizations.

Even better, she'd exceeded the council's expectations, which stopped just short of signing an oath in blood. *Her* blood, so she'd take the win like a champion.

If only she felt like a champion, instead of the biggest loser on the plant because of how badly she'd hurt Langston.

She looked down at her clipboard, staring at the checklist but not really seeing the words.

"Hello, dear." Chairperson Clydelle stepped up to the window, startling Sandra. The old woman leaned heavily against her cane.

"Good morning." Sandra smiled.

"You've done a fantastic job, just as I knew you would," said Clydelle.

Sandra's head snapped around. "Um, what?" Confidence wasn't at all the vibe Chairperson Clydelle had given off when Sandra pitched the idea to bring the extreme snowboarding championship to the city council. Or any other time for that matter.

Clydelle waved a gloved hand in the air. "Oh, I know I was hard on you, but I'm only that way when I see great potential. You have it."

Wait. *What?* "Potential?" Sandra thumbed her own chest. "Are you talking about me?"

Clydelle chuckled. "Of course, I'm talking about you. I've seen it in you for years. You just didn't see it in yourself until now. You're different. Something's changed. And it looks good on you."

A flash of color had Sandra turning back to the window. Regret vibrated through her as Langston emerged from the equipment storage room across from the lodge with the entire ski patrol following in their bright red jackets. With skis and poles bundled over their shoulders, they trudged into the opening where they had room to snap their high-tech ski boots into the bindings of their skis.

She hadn't done Langston any favors, as she'd foolishly thought she was doing. She'd hurt him terribly. A mistake she'd likely pay for dearly for years to come. Or however long it took for her to get over losing him. She'd tried to talk to him, but he wanted nothing to do with her. Had stayed distant and cold during the staff meetings and when they'd had to work together on the event.

Unless it was strictly professional, today wasn't the day to approach him again. Tomorrow might not be the right time either. Or next week, or next month, or next year. But someday, maybe he'd forgive her enough to at least let her apologize.

"I'm proud of the work I've done." But instead of pride, she felt sadness all the way to her bones.

Clydelle followed her gaze. "The love of a man makes us do

crazy things sometimes, but you're one of the most resilient people I've ever met. You'll figure it out."

Sandra shook her head. "I don't think so. It's too late."

A snowmobile pulled up in front of the lodge.

"A lot can happen in a day," said Clydelle. "That's my ride. I'll see you at the ceremony. The whole city council will be there." She waddled to the door, her cane clicking against the floor as she left.

Sandra watched the council chairperson climb onto the back of the snowmobile and hook her arms around the driver's waist. Clydelle waved over a shoulder as the snowmobile pulled away from the lodge.

Sandra turned her attention back to Langston.

His lips moved, and his ski patrol listened. When he was done talking, they put on their goggles or sunglasses and headed toward the bunny slope.

It was time. She drew in a deep breath, gathered her courage, and stuffed the clipboard into the backpack at her feet. Just as she slipped her arms into the shoulder straps, her phone rang.

She pulled it from her jacket pocket. "This is Sandra." She pressed the phone against her knit pink, gray, and black Neff winter beanie cap that covered her ears.

"Sandra! Will Carlisle here."

Ah, the International Snowboarding Association's representative who had been assigned to check in with Sandra on the event's progress. Really, he was mostly assigned to keep an eye on her and make sure she got the job done.

"Good morning, Mr. Carlisle. Everything okay?"

"Everything's perfect. You've done a spectacular job, which is why the ISA is insisting you get over to the ceremony early for a photo op. We're waiting for you by the ribbon."

She looked over at the bunny slope, where the crowd was growing ever larger.

"On my way." Without bothering to put on skis, she set out toward the ceremony. It wasn't far, and she was wearing heavy snow boots, so she could put skis on later when it was time to take the lift up to the course.

As she approached, the crowd of spectators parted, and Sandra realized for the first time that a large number of them were locals. Sure enough, the city council members were there, and the entire crowd began to...clap. For *her*.

Her throat closed.

She'd kept her focus solely on the shop and the event since the day she'd broken Langston's heart, afraid to face him or anyone else in town, retreating into her shell again like she'd done for so long. She'd assumed everyone would turn against her again.

As she walked through the large crowd, someone patted her on the back. "Good job, Sandra!"

She stopped, looked the man with graying temples in the eye, and said, "Thank you." Apparently, Langston hadn't told anyone. Then again, that wasn't his style. He'd kept secrets for her for so long, he wouldn't broadcast their personal business now because he was hurt. He wasn't that kind of guy.

The owner of Shear Elegance, Red River's most fashionable beauty salon, stepped into her path. "I just wanted to say thank you," Brianna said. "My shop is so dang busy with tourists, I'm working around the clock. The extra revenue that's pouring in will finally allow me to remodel the salon."

Oh, jeez. Sandra had made the thirty-minute drive to Taos once a month to avoid the salons in Red River because everyone knew they were the best place to catch up on gossip. Gossip was something she refused to participate in because she knew how hurtful it could be.

"My husband's business is booming, too, because of the extra tourists this event has attracted. Thank you." Brianna held out her hand.

"Um." Sandra looked at Brianna's gloved hand, as though she wasn't sure it was real. "You're..." Sandra's voice cracked. "You're welcome." Sandra finally managed to get the words out as she shook Brianna's hand.

Sandra had let a few bitter people overshadow all the good folks in this town. Why hadn't she seen it sooner? Before so many years were lost? Before the best person she'd ever met got hurt?

She glanced at the ski patrol grouped around Langston. They stood on the fringe of the crowd. With his sunglasses on, she couldn't make out his expression, but the line of his jaw was hard, and his lips were thinned.

When she stepped into the clearing, Mr. Carlisle waved her over. He stood with a smaller group of people behind the large red ribbon that stretched between two posts. A huge banner listing the event sponsors served as the backdrop. Sandra had worked with the sign company to design it herself because she'd wanted it to be perfect for the cameras that were covering the event. Once the two-day event was over, the trophies would be awarded in front of that banner, and the sponsors needed to be happy with the televised exposure.

Carlisle engulfed her hand with both of his and shook it as though she was someone important.

Pfsst.

When he introduced her to the other reps from the ISA as the rock star who saved this year's competition, she couldn't take it anymore. She wanted all the accolades to stop. For years she'd yearned for approval, but her cheeks were starting to burn.

"Let me introduce some of the others who've been instrumental in pulling this event together." Her gaze bounced around the crowd, but for the life of her she blanked. Couldn't spot the event staff besides Langston. "Um, well..."

Chairperson Clydelle used her cane to push through the group of ski patrollers and eased up beside Langston.

"I owe the city council my gratitude—"

"Nonsense!" shouted Clydelle.

Really? The woman claimed to be hard of hearing.

She tugged at Langston's sleeve. "Help me walk over there, young man. I'm not steady enough on my feet anymore to walk in this snow."

Without releasing the tension in his jaw, he held out an arm and escorted Clydelle over.

"There now," she said. "I won't have to shout, and I can certainly hear better."

Right.

Langston tried to withdraw his arm, at which point, the old woman latched on tighter.

He must've known that he was bested because he gave up and stayed at her side, with her arm linked through his.

Sandra would've laughed if her pulse wasn't pounding in her ears.

"What were you saying, Mr. Carlisle? I'd like to hear it before we take pictures," Clydelle all but cooed with innocence.

Which told Sandra she was anything but.

Just what *did* this sly old woman have up her sleeve?

Carlisle beamed and cleared his throat. "Sandra, Clydelle and I have been talking about your skill set. About how hard you've worked for years, even buying a failing business and turning it around." He hitched his chin at Clydelle. "She's a huge fan of yours, by the way."

Okaaay. News to Sandra. Until a few minutes ago in the lodge.

"You've done such an exceptional job with this event." He chuckled and shook his head. "Honestly, we weren't sure you'd be able to manage it, but it was worth a try rather than canceling the whole event."

Gee. She felt so special.

"I mean, I can't stress enough how impossible this project really was," Carlisle plowed on. "No matter who we hired, the odds of failure were better than good. Yet you pulled it off beautifully. You were obviously born to do this kind of work."

The rest of the ISA members nodded.

Well, hell. She really did feel a little special now. *But where is Carlisle going with this?*

He rubbed his hands together. "I know Red River is your

home. It's a beautiful place, and we know it would take a lot to get you to leave."

She nearly choked.

"But we'd like to offer you a job at our headquarters in Denver, and we'll make it worth your while if you'll at least hear us out after the event is over and consider our offer. I promise you, it's generous."

Sandra's lips parted, but the words wouldn't come.

The ISA was offering her a job. Financial security. A ticket out of Red River.

Everything she'd ever wanted. Except for...

Her gaze latched onto Langston.

His face didn't register any emotion.

A month ago, she would've jumped at an offer to leave Red River.

Now she was hoping Langston would offer her a reason to stay.

She waited a beat. Then another, her heart pounding so hard against her chest that she was sure others could hear it.

Besides a muscle ticking at his jaw, Langston didn't move.

Her heart split in half.

But she couldn't show it. Not today. So she forced a smile and turned to Mr. Carlisle to give him her answer. "I'll—"

Clydelle swooned. "Oh, dear. I'm not feeling well." She leaned against Langston. Then her eyes rolled back, and she floated toward the ground.

CHAPTER TEN

"Get a stretcher!" Langston yelled at his ski patrol team as he lowered Clydelle to the ground.

Two of them darted away, heading for the shed next to the lifts, where the basket stretchers were stored.

"Everyone, back away so the medical team has room." He reached into his pocket and pulled out a walkie-talkie. "Base camp, we need Doc Holloway at the bunny slope ASAP, and bring an ambulance around to the lodge." He tossed the device into the snow and went to work on his patient.

He loosened the scarf around her neck, then put two fingers against her neck.

Thank fuck, her pulse was strong and regular.

"Ms. Clydelle," he said gently, kneeling at her side.

Her eyes fluttered open. She blinked like she was trying to bring him into focus. Her wrinkled lips parted. "Sandra. I need Sandra."

All right, but not what he expected from an old woman who'd just collapsed. He had no idea Clydelle and Sandra had gotten so close. Then again, he obviously didn't know a lot of things about his ex-lover.

"Help is on the way," he said. "You need to save your strength. Don't talk unless you have to."

She closed her eyes as though she might never open them again. "I have to. I need Sandra."

Langston found Sandra in the crowd and hooked a finger at her.

She didn't walk, she ran.

"She's asking for you." Langston found Clydelle's pulse under the layers of winter clothes and gloves and checked it again. Still strong.

"Before I die, I want you two to talk things out." Her voice was a raspy whisper. "At least forgive each other if you can't patch things up."

Right now? She had to be kidding.

He gave her a smile to reassure her. "Clydelle, you're not going to die on my watch, but your health is more important right now than anything else." A siren buzzed for a split second, then shut off. That was Langston's cue that the ambulance was pulling up in front of the lodge.

"Coming through!" Ski patrol arrived with a basket stretcher dragging behind them.

Doc Holloway pushed through the crowd with a first aid backpack and joined Langston and Sandra at Clydelle's side. "Hey, Ms. Clydelle. Have you been taking your medicine?"

She nodded, batting eyelashes at Doc. "Of course."

"Good." He placed a hand on her shoulder. "Let's get you to the hospital."

"Not until I talk some sense into these two stubborn kids." Clydelle's voice got a little stronger. "And that's final."

Langston couldn't help but pull his brows together. The woman had just collapsed, and her biggest concern was to talk to him and Sandra?

"I won't be able to rest in peace unless I know I've done all I can to convince you both of what you should've known all along, so be a good boy, Doctor Holloway, and give me a few minutes with these two."

Doc looked skeptical, but he also must've known there was no use arguing because he glanced at his watch. "You've got two minutes." He stood. "And I'm only backing off a few steps."

"That's all I need." She gave Doc a few more bats of her lashes. Once Doc stepped away, she said low enough so only the three of them could hear, "You belong together. Why else would you have stayed together so many years?"

Sandra let a gasp slip through her lips. "You knew?"

"I know everything that goes on in this town, dear." Clydelle licked her lips as though her mouth was filled with cotton.

"Ms. Clydelle." Langston fought for patience. "We need to go to the hospital. We can talk later."

She shook her head as though she was weak, but her boney fingers fisting his sleeve to pull him closer had him narrowing his eyes. When she did the same to Sandra, he knew he'd been had.

"There's nothing wrong with you, is there?" he whispered.

"No." The old woman glanced toward the crowd. "But they don't know that. How awful would it look for the safety officer to walk away from an old woman who just fainted?"

"Oh, good grief." Sandra blew out a breath that said she was just as exasperated as him. "You pick now to intervene in my life?"

"Interfere would be my word of choice," said Langston.

Clydelle gave him a censuring look, then turned her attention to Sandra. "I've been *intervening* in your life for years. You just didn't know it."

When several creases appeared across the strip of Sandra's forehead that was exposed between her sunglasses and beanie cap, Clydelle went on to say, "Who do you think convinced the banker to give you the loan to buy the shop? You had no collateral other than a store that was already failing. Not exactly a sound investment from a loan officer's point of view." She let her head loll to the side, obviously still putting on a show for the bystanders.

"One minute," said Doc Holloway, his tone growing more urgent.

"You'll wait your turn, young man," said Clydelle.

Funny how she could shush a man over six feet tall with just a few words, because Doc crossed his arms and quieted.

"Convincing your landlord to hold off on putting your office space on the market until you came to your senses was a problem, but when I offered to send her on a paid vacation, that did the trick." She looked thoughtful. "But when Mr. Carlisle approached me for a reference because he was putting your name forward for a job at the ISA, that was a hard one." She pulled Langston closer. "I gave her a glowing recommendation because I thought for sure you'd ask her to stay."

Langston brushed a gloved hand over his jaw. "I never wanted her to go, that's the problem. She was going to go anyway."

"Don't tell me, hon." She pointed to Sandra. "Tell her."

He let his stare settle on Sandra. Really settle on her. She was beautiful. Always had been the most beautiful woman he'd ever known. After the landlord let it slip that Sandra had been planning to leave town without telling him, he'd walked away. Finally, that had been the last straw. He'd waited long enough and vowed to never waste another minute on her. Told himself he could find someone else to settle down with and start a family, like all of his friends had done.

But telling himself that and actually believing it were two very different things. He still loved her. Still wanted her. Still needed her.

He blew out a breath. "Sans, I—"

"Langston, don't." She held up a hand, and a tear slipped from under her shades. "Let me talk. You've done enough for me. You've waited patiently. Kept our relationship quiet and kept my...secrets about my father all to make me happy. You aren't the one who needs to explain or apologize for anything. I owe you an apology. I owe Red River an explanation because I've spent years hiding like the same scared little teenager I was in high school. I misled people. I didn't give anyone in this town a chance, but I especially didn't give you the life you deserved."

Langston waited. Weighed her words.

She rubbed a nervous hand up and down the leg of her snow pants.

"What were you going to tell Mr. Carlisle?" he finally asked. "Because I really need to know, Sans."

Another crease appeared across her forehead. "Um, what?"

"About the job. Were you going to take it and leave town after all?" His insides cinched tight and he realized he was afraid of the answer. Afraid it wouldn't be what he wanted to hear, but he'd played the game her way for too long and it was time to lay it all out on the table.

"It sounds like a great opportunity." The speed of her hand rubbing against her thigh increased.

The invisible rope tightening around Langston's heart tightened.

"But I wasn't going to take it."

He let his eyes slide shut and let out the breath he hadn't realized he was holding.

She shook her head, as though she couldn't believe her own words and chuckled. "I've been looking for a way out of this town since I was a teenager. When I finally got it, I couldn't leave. Not if there was the slightest chance that you might forgive me after you had time to cool off."

Doc Holloway stepped closer. "Time's up." He waved over the stretcher.

"Wait," Sandra said. "Before you go, why all this?" She waved a hand over Ms. Clydelle laying on the ground. "Why all the drama?"

Clydelle lifted a shoulder. "I like drama. At my age, it makes life more interesting. I also couldn't risk you taking the job when butthead here didn't speak up." She gave Langston another disapproving look.

Still, he couldn't fault her for looking out for him and Sandra. Her heart was in the right place.

And then it hit him.

Sandra's heart had been in the right place, too. Everything she'd done, she'd done for his benefit, because she was thinking of him.

Clydelle winked. "And I get an examination from Doc Holloway and an ambulance ride with some handsome paramedics." She waved Doc over. As they lifted her onto the stretcher, she said, "They don't call it the wise years for nothing. It's one of the only perks of living to be a ripe old age." She scrunched her wrinkly nose. "Well, that and vodka. It goes nicely with lemonade on a hot summer day. And Bailey's Irish cream for my coffee during the winter."

Ski patrol strapped her into the basket stretcher.

"What's a girl to do, now that the fire department has banned me from watching them wash the fire engine in the summer?" She shrugged. "I guess they didn't appreciate me offering to put a twenty in their utility belts if they'd take off their shirt."

The ski patroller pushed off and tugged her toward the lodge.

Thank God.

Sandra was still staring at the retreating stretcher with her jaw hanging open when Langston grasped her sleeve and pulled her into his arms.

"You are one stubborn ass woman, you know that?" He wrapped her in his arms, pulling her close. He wasn't going to ever to let her go again.

"I do know that." Another tear slipped down her cheek, rosy from the cold morning air.

He wiped it away.

"You have no reason to give me another chance." She sniffed.

He placed a gloved finger over her lips to shush her. "It's me that doesn't deserve a second chance. You thought you were protecting me, but I should've stood up for what I knew was right a long time ago and told everyone the truth. I wanted it to be your decision. I thought I was doing the right thing, but I wasn't."

He took her face in his hands and kissed her gently. Lovingly.

"Just so you know, you were never my dirty little secret, Langston." Her voice was a hushed whisper. "You've always been my soulmate. The only man I've ever loved. Which is the reason I was going to tell Mr. Carlisle that I don't need time to think about the job. I'm staying in red River. I don't want my life here to be over."

"Oh, babe." He brushed another kiss across her soft lips. "Our life together is just beginning." He took her mouth with his, and she tasted like warm coffee and cranberry pecan scone. Her kiss grew deeper and more intimate until she melted against him like she always did when they were alone and could show their true feelings for each other.

A throat cleared behind them.

Langston broke the kiss and leaned his forehead against hers.

"We seem to have forgotten we're in public." Nice. Their relationship would never be a secret again.

"Um, so I take it you're not interested in the job at the ISA?" asked Mr. Carlisle.

Sandra stepped out of Langston's embrace, but stayed at his side. "I'm sorry, but no, I'm not. I'd love to coordinate any winter sporting events your association wants right here, though. I'm happy to be your go-to person in Red River."

"I understand," said Carlisle. "I won't lie, though. I'm disappointed. You'd make a great addition to our team."

"Thank you for the vote of confidence, Mr. Carlisle." She glanced around the crowd. "But I love it here. Can you give me a second before we get the ribbon cutting ceremony underway?"

He nodded and walked away.

Sandra turned back to Langston. "I love you."

He encased her beautiful face with his hands, pressing a kiss to her forehead. "I love you, too."

"You're sure you want to be stuck with me?" She laughed, nuzzling her nose against his cheek.

"Damn sure," he said. "I want to be stuck with you forever. Will you finally make an honest man out of me?"

She nodded, a smile so bright that he felt it deep in his soul. "Yes."

"Good." He placed another kiss on her cheek, then used his teeth to pull off one glove, then the other. He tossed them into the snow alongside the walkie-talkie. Then he withdrew the velvet box he was still carrying around in his pocket. He'd called himself a schmuck for still putting it in his pocket every morning after he'd found out she'd planned to leave town.

His schmuckery was paying off, though.

He dropped to one knee and opened the box. "Sandra Edwards, will you mar—"

"Yes!" She grabbed the front of his jacket with both hands and hauled him to his feet. "Now get up here and kiss me and make it official."

"Sure thing, boss." He laid the hottest, sexiest, open-mouthed kiss on her, until she sighed into his mouth and had to lean into him for support.

Cheers and more clapping rang out from the crowd.

She tilted her head back to look up at him. "After years of wanting to keep us a secret, we're making out in front of the whole town with national broadcasters recording us." She smiled up at him, and he knew she was as lost in him as he was her. "And it feels perfect."

It *was* perfect.

He notched his chin toward the group of ISA members who were starting to look impatient. "Now that we've got forever to be together, we can take this up at home."

He didn't think it was possible for her smile to get brighter, but it did.

"Go get 'em, tiger." He released her and watched as she joined the fray.

Now that he finally had her—fully, completely—he really would rather take her home and celebrate their new engagement in private.

But they did have forever. Forever was a long time, and he planned to make every minute of it count.

* * *

Thank you for reading IT'S IN HIS FOREVER, the fifth book in my Red River series of STANDALONE novels and novellas.

If you loved Langston and Sandra's story, you'll love Dylan and Hailey's story just as much. Get it now by one-clicking here: IT'S IN HIS SONG

About IT'S IN HIS SONG, the next steamy standalone novella in the Red River Series:

They're both back in Red River for good, and the chemistry is stronger than ever. But will her secret tear them apart all over again?

Dylan McCoy is restless to take over Red River's favorite watering hole—Cotton Eyed Joe's—when his Uncle Joe retires. First, he's got to prove that he has what it takes to carry on Joe's legacy. Finally able to put the painful scars from his days working in L.A.'s trendy music scene behind him, he sets out to host a weekend workshop for song writers. He calls in a favor and lines up some of the biggest musicians in the biz to attend. Life is good. Until the business owners who occupy the commercial space next door threaten to ruin his establishment right before the rock star lineup of attendees are scheduled to blow into town.

Hailey Hicks left Red River six years ago with a secret. Now—as a seasoned hairstylist who's made her own way in the world—she's back in town to help her cousin expand her salon. Unfortunately, the renovations aren't going as planned and draw fire from the saloon next door. When she comes face to face with her ex, Dylan McCoy, sparks fly. Can they mend the damage done because of how they parted ways? Or will her secret cause them both to get burned again?

If you haven't read the rest of the series, One-Click IT'S IN HIS HEART and see where it all began!

Sign up for my VIPeep Reader List to find out about new books, awesome giveaways, and exclusive content including excerpts and deleted scenes: SHELLY'S VIPEEP READER LIST

I pinky swear to never, ever share your email addy with anyone, and I only send out newsletters when I've got exciting news about a sale, a new book, or awesome giveaways.

And don't miss my DARE ME Series! Set on the picturesque vacation island of Angel Fire Falls, it's a sizzling series about secrets and second chances.

One-Click DARE ME ONCE!

Do you like more steam in your romance novels? Try my super sizzling series of erotic rom coms.

Download FOREPLAY now.

About the Checkmate Inc. Series:

Leo Foxx, Dex Moore, and Oz Strong spent their youths studying a chessboard, textbooks... and women, from afar. Now they're players in the city that never sleeps. Gone are their shy demeanors, replaced with muscle, style, and enough sex appeal to charm women of all ages, shapes, and cup sizes. They've got it all, including a multimillion-dollar business called Checkmate Inc.—a company they founded together right out of college.

Some guys are late bloomers, but once they hit their stride, they make up for lost time.

And the bonus? The founding partners of Checkmate Inc.

didn't become successful and smokin' hot by accident. They were smart enough to surround themselves with guys who helped them transform into the men they are today. So get ready for more stories about the hotties who are connected to Checkmate Inc.

A fun, flirty, and dirty contemporary series in which the sizzling hot players associated with Checkmate Inc. meet their matches.

Reviews are an author's best friend! They spread the word to others who enjoy the same books as you. So be sure to leave a review for IT'S IN HIS FOREVER on AMAZON, B&N, GOODREADS, BOOKBUB and any other favorite sites.

ALSO BY SHELLY ALEXANDER

Shelly's titles with a little less steam (still sexy, though!):

The Red River Valley Series

It's In His Heart – Coop & Ella's Story

It's In His Touch – Blake & Angelique's Story

It's In His Smile – Talmadge & Miranda's Story

It's In His Arms – Mitchell & Lorenda's Story

It's In His Forever - Langston & His Secret Love's Story

It's In His Song - Dylan & Hailey's Story

It's In His Christmas Wish - Ross & Kimberly's Story

The Angel Fire Falls Series

Dare Me Once — Trace & Lily's Story

Dare Me Again — Elliott & Rebel's Story

Dare Me Now — TBA

Dare Me Always — TBA

Shelly's sizzling titles (with a lot of steam):

The Checkmate Inc. Series

ForePlay – Leo & Chloe's Story

Rookie Moves – Dex & Ava's Story

Get Wilde – Ethan & Adeline's Story

Sinful Games – Oz & Kendall's Story

Wilde Rush - Jacob & Grace's Story TBA

ABOUT THE AUTHOR

Shelly Alexander is the author of contemporary romances that are sometimes sweet, sometimes sizzling, and always sassy. A 2014 Golden Heart® finalist, a 2019 RITA® finalist, and a 2019 HOLT Medallion finalist, she grew up traveling the world, earned a bachelor's degree in marketing, and worked in the business world for twenty-five years. With four older brothers and an older sister, she watched every *Star Trek* episode ever made, joined the softball team instead of ballet class, and played with G.I. Joes while the Barbie Corvette stayed tucked in her closet. When she had three sons of her own, she decided to escape her male-dominated world by reading romance novels and has been hooked ever since. Now she spends her days writing steamy contemporary romances while tending to two toy poodles named Mozart and Midge.

Be the first to know about Shelly's new releases, giveaways, appearances, and bonus scenes not included in her books! Sign up for her Reader List and receive VIP treatment:
shellyalexander.net

Other ways to stalk Shelly:
BookBub
Amazon
Email

A Touch of Sass, LLC

This book is a work of fiction. All names, characters, locations, and incidents are products of the author's imagination. Any resemblance to actual persons living or dead, things, locales, or events is entirely coincidental.

Cover design by Fiona Jayde Media

Editing by Alicia Carmical

Print ISBN: 978-0-9979623-3-8

❀ Created with Vellum

CPSIA information can be obtained
at www.ICGtesting.com
Printed in the USA
LVHW092040061219
639737LV00004B/539/P